Francis Dehaut de Pressense, E Ingall

Cardinal Manning

Francis Dehaut de Pressense, E. Ingall

Cardinal Manning

ISBN/EAN: 9783337060152

Printed in Europe, USA, Canada, Australia, Japan

Cover: Foto ©Raphael Reischuk / pixelio.de

More available books at **www.hansebooks.com**

CARDINAL MANNING

FROM THE FRENCH

OF

FRANCIS DE PRESSENSÉ

BY

E. INGALL

LONDON
WILLIAM HEINEMANN
1897

CARDINAL MANNING

INTRODUCTION

THESE pages, written for a Review,[1] aimed at presenting, in a necessarily imperfect shape, a slight sketch of one of the loftiest and noblest Christian figures of this century. They are now reproduced unchanged, but in a more permanent form, partly in obedience to kindly advice and too highly flattering requests, but more especially because I wished to answer certain criticisms to which these modest articles have given rise.

Were I to consult only my own wishes, and, I will add, my own interests, I should most probably do better in not seeking to prolong the naturally ephemeral existence of a production called forth by a special occasion. When one has cherished for long,

[1] They appeared under the title—"Manning.—I. Les Années Protestantes ; II. Les Années Catholiques," in the *Revue des Deux Mondes*, May 1 and 15, 1896.

B

the hope of some day writing the history of a great religious movement, a hasty and incomplete sketch is hardly the right method of fulfilling the project. No one can be more fully aware than I am of the defects and gaps that disfigure this present study, of its imperfections, inherent perhaps through the narrow limits or the rapidity of the narration; imperfections, too, which I ought perhaps easily to have avoided. I do not claim to give here a full-length portrait of Cardinal Manning, nor, above all, a portrait worthy in every detail of that great model. Still less am I under the delusion that I have offered even a summary explanation of the origin and progress of Anglo-Catholicism.

In this Essay, as in all those with biographical subjects, there is, if I may venture to say so, at once more and less than in a chapter of History; less, because the subject is not a great party or a whole generation, but a single individual; more, because nothing can equal the infinite complexity, the inexhaustible riches of a man's soul, and it is exactly those which I propose to depict. The valuable sympathy called forth by the publication of these pages has encouraged me, perhaps imprudently, to re-issue them in a new form. This sympathy has been due, I feel sure, to the human, pathetic, and dramatic elements in the figure of Cardinal Manning. The severe criticisms, the harsh reproofs that have not been spared me, have clearly been due to the insufficiency of my powers to do full justice to this great subject. Nevertheless, I should not dare to affirm that there are no traces in these criticisms of that narrowness of mind and heart, those sectarian prejudices that seem to me more out of place here than anywhere else.

I was by no means ignorant of what I was doing, nor of what I might expect, in rendering homage, as conspicuously as I knew how, to this man, one of those who, emerging from Protestantism, have the most contributed to the restoration of Catholicism as a spiritual power, and to the triumph of the so-called Ultramontane doctrines. Nothing could seem to me more natural, more legitimate even, than the surprise or the irritation of certain minds. I had foreseen certain objections, even certain protests, in the name of the principles of the Reformation.

There are three lines of attack, any one of which a Protestant critic might have fairly taken. First, without entering into a detailed examination of the facts on which I believed I could found my admiration, respect, and veneration for Cardinal Manning, he might have contented himself by asking me as an opening question, how I could reconcile my state of mind with a profession of Protestantism. Secondly, differing from my interpretation of known documents, or appealing to fresh ones, he might have contested the evidence in hand, and object to my description and judgment of the importance of the events of Manning's inner and outer life. Thirdly, putting the biography entirely aside, he might have taken up separately for discussion or refutation the principles explicitly or implicitly put forward in these pages, the foregone conclusions which betray themselves, the sympathies or antipathies which are disclosed, the judgments which are passed on men and things of the two Churches. If either of these critics, bringing together all these data, drawing from these premisses their logical conclusions, had delighted in bringing into contrast and into contradiction what he believed he found in my articles, that positively affirmed or involuntarily avowed my opinions on the gravest subjects, with what he knew about my acknowledged convictions or even my inmost feelings, I might have regretted a certain want of justice, deplored some absence of tact, contested some deductions, combated certain arguments, even refused to some the right to judge, but it would have been impossible for me to complain of a method of polemics so respectful to the conscience of the adversary.

The error might have been on one side or the other, perhaps on both, but the spirit of contention and chicanery, the implicit assertion of moral superiority, would have been absent. God forbid that I should be so ungrateful as to assert that I have met only with bitter antagonists! I cannot forget the exquisite delicacy, the discreet attitude of men whom I have been accustomed to venerate as authoritative examples of living Christianity, and who, forced by their consciences to point out errors fatal in their eyes, have done it with a moderation, a patience, a breadth of view, a charity for which I shall be for ever grateful. I could mention public writers, religious authors, who, while far from endorsing my opinions, have not considered it their duty or their right to hurl the thunderbolts of excommunication, to condemn in the mass and without right of appeal, to claim the possession of superior enlightenment about facts or persons without the materials for an independent opinion; finally, to give to the public, as news worthy of credence, gratuitous inventions of their own brains and of those alone.

Such articles as that in the *Journal Religieuse de la Suisse Romande* clearly show that there is a method of controversy in which the most uncompromising fidelity to Protestant principles is compatible with Christian charity. The writer of that article possesses an hereditary tradition of truthfulness, amenity, and justice, but such generous treatment cannot be expected from every one.

At the same time, why am I compelled to take notice of attacks made in such a different spirit? One of them begins by covering his face at the mere sight of the scandal caused by a born Protestant speaking with sympathy and admiration of a fugitive from Protestantism. He is indignant at the effrontery of a writer who dares to protest against Mr. Purcell's method of writing history, Mr. Purcell having been suddenly promoted to the first rank of authors, and declared a pure, undefiled fountain-head of information. According to this critic, there is an intolerable lack of propriety and even of good faith in taking from the book of the self-styled biographer of Cardinal Manning the proofs of the numberless errors of fact, and of the incomparably grosser and more culpable errors of judgment with which this singular painter has disfigured the features and degraded the expression of his model.

Critics who have probably not taken the trouble to read and especially to study carefully the 1600 pages of Mr. Purcell's massive book, do not admit the right of passing a severe judgment upon a work which has been sufficiently recommended to them by its disparagement of one of the great men of modern Catholicism. Mr. Purcell's two volumes are full of insinuations and accusations against Cardinal Manning. That is enough; they come from a master-workman's hand ; they must be accepted as gospel; and to point out the gross faults, the monstrous contradictions, the astonishing examples of ignorance, the constant falsifying of dates, the inaccurate quotations, the unfairly used documents, the confusion of thought, the vulgarity of style, and worse than all, the spirit of disparagement which makes this work a pitiful example of all that a biography worthy of the name should not be,—to point out all these things is to lay oneself open to the charge of prejudice in favour of the Church of Rome, and of treason towards the Reformation!

But this is not all. Such defenders of Protestant orthodoxy go farther. Not content with rummaging with a rather heavy hand in the most private and most sacred recesses of a man's conscience, our journalist takes upon himself the attributes of a prophet. In an official fashion, as if he could not doubt it, or rather as if he had received an express command to do so, he announces as an accomplished fact, a conversion or an abjuration which is merely the logical conclusion that he has chosen to draw from the premisses laid down by himself. He is so sure of his facts, that he comments upon this piece of news he has just announced, and which, he declares, in impressive tones, he would gladly not believe. Then begins a regular comedy.

The information thus circulated is caught up by the thousand echoes of journalism. After the religious Press comes the lay Press, then even the lightest Society papers. Comments are freely made. The rumour gains fresh strength at each stage of its progress. Soon, those very people who have taken this liberty of playing with their opponent's name, find they have a grievance against him. It has pleased them out of their certain knowledge to attribute to him an act that is too important and concerns too closely the domain of conscience for its authenticity to remain unconfirmed. They are angry with him for his silence. If he decline to accept this arbitrary judgment, he is reproached with want of respect for the public; he is expected to answer questions that should not have been asked. If he does not consent to give back *quid pro quo*, he will be summarily treated. Has he the weakness to cherish some unfashionable prejudice against the violation of the soul's modesty, does he positively refuse to bring into the full light of publicity, not merely his actions, words, thoughts, but also the innermost struggles and most secret anguish of his mind, he will be plainly shown that he is wrong, and that the Press has the right to learn—or rather, to know all.

Thus are perpetuated the old methods, adapted to our softer manners of to-day. Thank God, the tribunal of the Inquisition no longer exists, but is one quite sure that some of its methods have not survived, and that they are not sometimes practised in the name and for the profit of the religion of free inquiry, of individualism and of liberty of conscience? There is, I must confess, something piquant in seeing oneself excommunicated by Geneva,—that is, banished from the communion of the Invisible Church by its official champions, under the pretext of a too marked predilection for the Visible Church. The paradox would be entertaining, if it were merely a question of making merry over the inconsistencies of one's judges.

Unhappily, these polemical writers find their echoes outside in many straightforward natures and simple minds. To meet all this gossip by silence would require an evenness of soul bordering very closely on the indifference of selfishness. Through silence, a man runs the risk of becoming an object of scandal. Therefore I think I ought to reply to attacks which, if I alone were concerned, I should perhaps leave unanswered. I pay no heed to those zealots for *pure and spotless religion* who, while omitting to add their names, have fired at me a volley of pious insults. I certainly do not include with these anonymous writers those champions of the Gospel who take to themselves the right of flinging in a man's face his most sacred memories, and of passing judgment on his filial piety, but I may be pardoned if I show some feeling in my reply.

In fact, what do they know of the heritage of true Liberalism, of breadth of views as well as of faith, left me by my father, Edmond de Pressensé? What do these know, who find pleasure in invoking and in turning to their own purposes against me the memory of him who has been sometimes called the Protestant Montalembert? Assuredly I know better than they the inviolable, inflexible, lifelong fidelity which he showed to the Church of his choice. I know how full of the spirit of individualistic Protestantism was that Christianity that sustained him in a cruel agony through eighteen months; I know, in those last weeks, when he was called on to practise what he had believed, how the principles of his chosen master, Alexandre Vinet, acquired in his eyes a fresh degree of evidence, and with what severity, even, he thought it right to judge certain recent developments of Catholicism.

Never has the idea occurred to me of appealing to certain unpremeditated phrases that dropped from his lips, but which others have not scrupled to use, and whose tendency seemed to predict the failure of the Reformed Church in France. I do not even recall the virulent attacks brought upon this intrepid champion of liberty of conscience, by his energetic attitude in the Senate towards anti-clerical tyranny, with its Articles 7, its expulsion of the religious orders, its shameful suppression of the grants to public worship, and its watchword—"Les Curés sac au dos!" All that I claim—and on this point, I confess, I allow neither opposition nor reply—is, to be allowed to draw my inspiration, if not from all my father's opinions, at least from his spirit, as I understand it. Let me invoke one of the noblest and most generous injunctions that he bequeathed to his children, by which he warned them never to allow a feeling due to his memory to become an obstacle to any belief adopted on sufficient grounds.

So long as I am guided by my conscience, so long as, popular or unpopular, the opinions I embrace weigh with me through their seeming conformity with the truth, and through that alone, so long as the voice that I shall try to hear and follow is that of Christ, I cannot attach a tragic importance to divergencies of views that are necessarily secondary. After all, perhaps the only important agreement is, not that which exists about fundamental matters of thought, but rather, the harmony of souls, the right direction of the will, the ear inclined and the spirit awake to the voice of revelation. The rest cannot be of capital importance, and that conception of the obligations of filial piety which insists on the duty of holding the same views on the question of authority and the Apostolic succession, must indeed be a strange one.

As a matter of fact, these personalities arise from a zeal whose origin I can respect, just as I have no grudge against good people who have informed me of their displeasure at seeing me judge favourably "an agent of Rome," who have reproached me with my ignorance, by informing me that *Protestant nations are far more prosperous than Catholic ones*, and who advised me to read a book upon the conflicts between Science and Faith, in which Catholicism was so completely shattered by arguments drawn from the arsenal of average free-thought, that nothing of Christianity was left standing. But it suffices that upright natures and consciences whose purity reflects Christ's religion have been troubled, saddened, and made anxious; and I am therefore bound to offer every explanation compatible with what is due to truth.

Since some, in whose good faith I have implicit belief, have been shocked at my treatment of the author of the life of Cardinal Manning and of his work, I feel I owe them a fuller justification of my views on Mr. Purcell and his book than I could give in my articles, even though their interest in such a client seems strange to me. Since others have been astonished at the very choice of this subject, and at seeing the figure of Manning sketched with such tender respect by an author who, at any rate, cannot be accused of having been educated in the cloister, I wish to give a rapid explanation of my reasons for having done so.

Since, finally, several of my critics have asked me point-blank questions about my own religious convictions, since they have tried every means, either to make me contradict myself and convict me of Catholicizing dilettanteism, or else to compel me in the future to complete the evolution they have calculated for me, and accept the syllogism that they have formulated, by admitting, like them, the necessity for one of those acts that can never be undone and by completing my abjuration, I owe it to them, to myself, to reproduce as faithfully as possible the state of mind that produced these articles—and, until now, these alone.

BEFORE dealing with any other point, it is best that I should explain myself in the matter of Mr. Purcell, the author of those two ponderous volumes of Manning's Life that have been the cause and the subject of my articles. The judgment that I passed upon him in the *Revue des Deux Mondes*, and that I feel bound to maintain in this volume, is so severe and differs so completely from that of some of my critics, that I should expose myself to the most pitiless verdict if I did not try to give sound reasons for it. In the short article to which I was limited, I could not enter into details in my criticism; I had to be satisfied briefly to show the characteristics of Mr. Purcell's mode of writing history, and proceed by a series of affirmations instead of by the slower process of proofs.

Several of my censors have been much displeased with me for this. I fancy they would have found it somewhat difficult to justify the sympathetic, almost tender interest, that they feel in Mr. Purcell. It has

really been a piece of good fortune for people, ill-
disposed towards Manning, to meet with such a
biographer, Catholic in creed, giving himself out as
authorized, almost as being appointed to the post;
a man who had incontestably drawn from the most
authentic sources, who undoubtedly brought a mass
of fresh documents, and who, whilst constantly
asserting his love, his respect for his hero, showered
on him discredit and shame through his narrative,
his opinions, his accusations, even through his
praises. Is it not, on the other hand, intolerable
that a writer whose antecedents would, *à priori*,
mean impartiality, and who can scarcely be accused of obeying preconceived sympathies, should
come in and spoil everything?

It would have been difficult to bring as a complaint against me, that I had not blindly accepted
the statements of this self-styled Catholic historian,
that I would neither accept his facts without verify-
ing them, nor endorse his opinions without examin-
ing them. What has brought upon me this severe
blame, has been my effrontery in pretending to
remonstrate with my master about these things, my
shamelessness in borrowing the chief materials for
my article from a book that I was treating so
badly. Truly this is a strange reproach! as if
there could be the smallest logical contradiction or
the slightest moral indelicacy in using documents
after passing them through the sieve of criticism,

in order to confront an author with himself, before putting him to use, and to ask him for the means of correction or refutation of his statements!

Besides, this is by no means an isolated book upon this subject. Mr. Purcell's biography has merely taken its place in the list of already numerous works; the titles of some of the chief of these were mentioned at the head of my first article. Manning himself had already given rise to a fairly rich literature. The extraordinary disdain with which this surprising biographer has treated alike the authors who preceded him and the works of Manning himself, is not one of the smallest sources of complaint against him. An historian who can make no use of the little volume by Mr. Hutton, or of the short but solid pamphlet in which Dr. Gasquet has given such an admirable sketch of the spiritual physiognomy of Cardinal Manning; a writer who does not search for a single piece of information in the sermons, prefaces, or other numerous productions from the pen of the Archbishop of Westminster during an active life of sixty years, betrays a singular lack of preparation for his task.

Happy would it be if he had committed only this grave sin of omission! Mr. Purcell will not owe a debt of gratitude to his champions; it is they who force us to bring forward the proofs of our accusations and to reveal to the public what is hidden by the sham verdicts of this self-styled judge of Cardinal Manning, and on what they rest. Let us first speak of the spirit in which Mr. Purcell has approached his task. He says very justly that "for a biographer, his hero should be the object of a special, a supreme interest"; we would add, of a respectful sympathy. Without that disposition, he had better leave to another the accomplishment of such a mission. And I venture to assert that Mr. Purcell is especially lacking in that quality.

Either he has long cherished an unfavourable prejudice against Manning, or he belongs to that class of mind which is incapable of feeling a lasting, loyal admiration for any one, and that soon wearies of giving the epithet "Just" to Aristides. Be that as it may, when studying Manning's life or telling its story, he betrays, one might almost say, a pre-conceived and growing enmity against him. It would be impossible to quote all the passages that reveal this state of mind; some typical examples will suffice to give an idea of it. He accuses Manning of the most grievous acts of pettiness whilst he was yet a child, and before his character was formed. When at school, he tells us, Manning never spoke of others, either in his letters or in his diary, but, on the other hand, he was ever ready to discourse minutely about himself.[1] At the University he attributes to him, along with a

[1] Vol. I. p. 18.

vanity that extended to his dress, an egotism, an exaggerated self-consciousness that, according to our author, stuck to him like the shirt of Nessus, to the end of his life.[1]   He mentions that, at that time, Manning troubled himself less about religious than about political questions, and makes the amiable remark that the young man could speak only of subjects that secured him an audience hanging on his lips.[2]   He writes, apparently unconscious of the harm that such an assertion, if true, would do to its object : "Circumstance, 'that unspiritual god,' before whom Manning had acquired the habit of bowing, demanded once more from its servant homage and sacrifice."[3]   He mentions in a passing remark, as the most ordinary thing possible, "the habit, partly natural, partly acquired by Manning," of never identifying himself with an unpopular movement, and never going over to a falling cause.[4]   Further on, he represents Manning as a man who never hesitated to sacrifice any friendship, when it was a question of the Church or of his *personal interest*.[5]

In a truly typical passage, he depicts this new Machiavelli, this Anglican Jesuit, as much more careful to serve his party by action at headquarters than by controversy at Oxford. To the ecclesiastical statesman, what were the subtleties of theology, the study of the Fathers, the claims or

[1] Vol. I. p. 30.　　[2] *Ibid.* p. 61.　　[3] *Ibid.* p. 195.
[4] *Ibid.* p. 204.　　　　　　　　　[5] *Ibid.* p. 244.

disclosures of Catholic antiquity, compared with the unloosing of the locks of action at Westminster? What the effects of Tract 90 towards the revival of Catholic life in the Church of England, compared to the granting by the Crown of self-government to the Church? What the pulpit of St. Mary's, Oxford, to the antechamber of a Minister in Downing Street?[1] According to him, Manning was the worshipper of the rising sun, the enemy of unpopular minorities, the born deserter of lost causes.

It seems to me, that the reproduction of these astonishing passages should greatly embarrass their author. How, if this description is correct, did Mr. Purcell conceive the idea of writing the life of this courtier of fortune, this ambitious man, this Church intriguer? How, especially, did he think he could make of him a hero and a saint? By what marvellous conjuring does he hope to reconcile these opinions flung out in passing, with the formula of canonization which crowns his work?

I leave to Mr. Purcell the task of reconciling these contradictions. It is enough for me to compare these calumnies with the facts (I mean those shown us by our author), and with the documents which he had at his disposal and has laid before us. The reader will doubtless not consider the word "calumnies" too strong when

[1] Vol. I. p. 265.

he has followed me in one or two of these investigations.

Let us begin with Manning's ordination. To describe this important event, Mr. Purcell consulted a certain number of papers which he has published in his usual strange way, as I will show later on, but has at least laid before us. The materials consisted of three autobiographical notes, drawn up by the Cardinal about fifty years after the date of the fact to which they refer, and, on the other hand, letters and fragments of letters written, from 1832, to his mother and to Mr. Twistleton, a friend of his youth. It is as clear as day from the contents of these documents that Manning, whether at the very time or half-a-century later, had an absolute conviction of obeying a call from Heaven, an appeal, as he himself said, from God *ad veritatem et ad se ipsum.* Everything testified to this ; there is not the shadow of a proof of the contrary. Mr. Purcell would surely consider himself bound to follow this version, the sole authentic one.

But not so. He insinuates that Manning's vocation was very probably the result of an illusion ; that the young clergyman deceived himself if he believed he was obeying other considerations than purely worldly motives, and that he did not really experience any of the religious emotions whose effect upon his soul he described later. This is speaking plainly.

It would be interesting to know what is the
foundation for all this structure of hypotheses, and
where are the documents allowing our author thus
to give the lie to his hero. Documents! There
are none. Mr. Purcell has merely considered *so
strange and extraordinary a motive as a divine
vocation* to be improbable and absurd. Forgetting
the two undeniably contemporary letters which he
has himself published, and which confirm in all
points the later version of the diary, he maintains
that the Cardinal, after time had past, had lost the
exact remembrance of the way in which things had
happened, and had slightly exaggerated matters.
If this argument does not convince the reader, he
has in reserve one which he believes to be irresistible; if Manning, he says, had really heard that
call, he would infallibly have communicated it to
his confidential friend, his daily correspondent,
his brother-in-law, Mr. John Anderdon. He has
not done this; therefore he did not obey this
supernatural impulse.

The syllogism is perfect. Mr. Purcell's logic is
faultless. The pity is, that his minor term is false.
Manning had positively acquainted his brother-in-
law with the feelings which moved him. There
exists a copy of his letters in two little manuscript-
books that have escaped Mr. Purcell. Dr. Gasquet,
who married the Cardinal's niece, had quoted, at
pages 10 and 11 of his short pamphlet, published in

1895, two extracts which finally dispose of all Mr. Purcell's statements. If the author of the pretended authorized biography had deigned to cast his eyes on this modest and admirable little work, he would have there found not only such information as this, drawn from the fountain-head, but also a luminous and delicate analysis of the spiritual nature of Cardinal Manning. *Ab uno disce omnes.* Such is the spirit in which the self-styled official biographer has approached his task!

It is this same singular inclination to disparagement that has guided him in his fashion of describing and judging another episode. This is Manning's refusal, in 1846, of the post of Sub-Almoner to the Queen, which had been offered to him when his brother-in-law, Samuel Wilberforce, was raised to the Episcopate. This post was the first rung in the ladder of honours. It would have brought him into connection with the Court, would have facilitated that rapid promotion which every one prophesied for him, and which would have been a strong temptation had he been the ambitious man his enemies and his biographer take him for. His diary of that time shows that after a week's reflection, he deliberately refused this offer, and tells us his motives for the refusal, viz. his parish duties, his need of inner mortification, and the more important interests of his soul. " To learn to say No," he wrote in these pages (kept for himself alone), "to disappoint myself, to choose the hardest way, to resist my inclinations, to prefer that people should think less well of me, to have fewer of this world's gifts; that cannot be wrong; it is too much like the Cross. Oh! humility, nothing but humility! May God grant it to me." Will it be believed? After having seen this passage, after having told us of the decision and what led to it, Mr. Purcell takes upon himself to instruct Manning in renunciation and humility. He unsparingly taxes him with ambition and worldliness. He attributes to him regrets that he chooses to consider due to remorse or to restlessness of temperament, or to both.

However strange, when compared with the original documents, may be this way of writing history, we have so far dealt only with comparative trifles. Having made such a good beginning, Mr. Purcell has not stopped short. He accuses Manning point-blank of having been deceitful in attitude and language from 1846 to 1851; with having hidden for six years from his Church and his best friends the state of his soul, and his inmost feelings; with having, in a word, covered with a veil of the most odious hypocrisy the great spiritual workings that were to lead him to the Catholic Church. If this reproach has any foundation, it blights and dishonours, not only this part of Manning's life, but his whole existence; his whole nature, his whole being are spotted with the most repulsive duplicity. His most cherished convictions, his charity, even his holiness, have their roots in a lie. One must renounce the vain attempt to set up for the admiration of men a master of the perfidious art of equivocal words and of acts with a double purpose. It is incomprehensible that Mr. Purcell should have wasted his time in raising a monument to one of whom he entertained such an opinion. It is a surprising contradiction. Does the author of this accusation feel its gravity so slightly, that he seems to throw it out at random without pausing to weigh its consequences? Thank Heaven! its proofs are totally lacking—or rather, everything agrees to refute this calumny.

Let us turn to a justly respected paper whose views are fully Anglican, and which has no prejudices in favour of those who have left the National Church, the *Spectator.* " In private diaries and letters," it says, " purporting to give what Mr. Purcell calls the ' inner man,' who doubted the validity of the Anglican position from the year 1846 to the year 1850, we find likewise his suspicion that the doubt may be due to delusion. This being so, he declares it to be his duty to speak hopefully of the English Church, and not to unsettle others in their allegiance to it. And in the letters cited in the same chapter as giving the 'outer man,' or the 'public voice,' we do *not* find assertions inconsistent with private doubts of the Anglican position, but rather a line of argument which urges the duty of remaining in the Anglican Communion in spite of personal doubts."[1]

This could not be better said, and this testimony of a competent and impartial critic will doubtless weigh in the mind of the reader against the imputations suggested by an incredible confusion of thought to a self-styled friend. The *Spectator*, like myself, considers the honesty of Manning as inviolable during that long, difficult, and dangerous period, when it was scarcely possible for him to bring into his language and attitude more unity than existed in his spiritual conceptions.

I shall hardly be required to examine minutely the strange tissue of errors and sophisms on which Mr. Purcell has based his statements. I will merely point out that in a statement where dates are necessarily of vital importance, Mr. Purcell assigns with hopeless carelessness, on the same page, at a few lines' distance, two different dates, 1847 and 1849, to a letter; a few pages farther on, he again gives this same letter another date, and completely. travesties its meaning to support his contention.

Has he adopted a more conscientious method

[1] *Spectator*, February 8, 1896.

25

when he comes to the Catholic years of Manning, that is to say, to that part of his career for which it may be supposed our author has most sympathy, and for which he is better prepared?

Far from it. There is again evident the temptation to sully his hero. He conveys the impression that Manning mixed himself up *proprio motu* in the affair of the coadjutor *cum jure successionis* of Cardinal Wiseman, that it was he who stirred up the dispute, waged war to the knife, and pursued in it his own ends. At the risk of seriously falsifying the true character of the two episcopates, Mr. Purcell has given a most disproportionate space to this episode, nearly two hundred pages of his second volume; why then has he not found room to say that Manning had been officially charged by his Archbishop to watch this matter in the Roman court, that he obeyed his superior's command, and that he could not do otherwise?

What an unfortunate falsification to represent the correspondence between Manning and Monsignor George Talbot as a kind of intrigue formed by an ambitious man, desirous of gaining the Pope's ear, and unscrupulous as to the means employed. Did Mr. Purcell know, or did he not, that the Pope's Chamberlain was the regular, recognized, normal organ of communications that did not pass through the College of the Propaganda, that he was the accredited agent of Cardinal Wiseman at the

Vatican, and that Manning, in writing to him, merely obeyed and followed the example of all his colleagues on the Archiepiscopal Staff?

These are very strange, very suspicious instances of forgetfulness. It is true that they lose their prominence in the presence of the culpable, free-and-easy fashion with which the self-styled author-ized biographer has thrown to the public the confidential notes of a secret correspondence, has shocked some and wounded others by reviving old quarrels, and has mischievously isolated all Manning's letters.

Since he has not found time to expatiate on the diocesan, spiritual, and charitable activity, on the preaching, on the work as director of consciences, on the books and works of Manning, yet was bent on writing so fully the history of this conflict, he ought, at least, to have completed the picture by retracing the final pacification. Is it like the im-partiality of an historian, to say nothing of the kindliness of a friend, to relate at full length the dispute between Manning and Canon Maguire, their sharp words, their sometimes hostile methods, and to omit all mention of their reconciliation, of that long illness during which the Archbishop daily visited his former adversary, who on his death-bed exclaimed—"Your footsteps on my staircase have been like music to my ear"? After having shown the painful conflict of Wiseman with his coadjutor

27

Errington, ought he not also to have described the noble serenity with which the former Archbishop of Trebizond retired to a small rural parish, and forgot, in the care of souls in that obscure village, the grandeur which had nearly fallen to his lot?

It is surely a pity to be silent about noble incidents like this, which, fairly used, add much to the value of biography.

What then of the inspiration which prompted the endless account of the misunderstandings between Newman and Manning? Mr. Purcell, from end to end, exalts the man whose life he is not writing, and belittles him who is supposed to be his hero. His partiality even breaks out so violently that it becomes its own antidote. He can see nothing wrong in the Oratorian of Edgbaston, nor can he find a meritorious action in the Archbishop of Westminster.

Happily here, the matter is infinitely superior to the mediocrity of our historian, who in his imperturbable fashion passes judgment on everything. It is too evident that it is not for him to settle such differences,

Tantas componere lites.

There are plenty of documents; he has added a whole cargo to those which were already forth-. coming. I am sure that the competent public will discern the truth, that it will disentangle the cause of this deplorable misunderstanding, that it will take into consideration circumstances, personal feelings, and surroundings, and that it will by no means endorse the unjust condemnation passed upon Manning by a man as incapable of reading his soul and understanding his nature as of entering into intimacy with Newman.

The evil is not perhaps very great ; still, critics paid by the hour or by the article, always on the watch for some happy chance to free them from reading a book before reviewing it, have made the most extravagant use of this interlude; and sectarian writers, ever fond of scandals in a rival Church, have vied with each other in moralizing upon this edifying spectacle of the quarrel between the two restorers of English Catholicism. If the public had not taken literally the noisy puffs by which Mr. Purcell and his friends had announced the publication of his book—

Nescio quid majus nascitur Iliade !

if they had not simply believed in the rather too presuming claims of our author, all these acts of perfidy would have had but little importance.

It will not be out of place to note that Cardinal Manning showed his usual kindliness in giving an authorization to Mr. Purcell to write his life.

So far-reaching was the great prelate's influence —so vast in effect was his life, extending through long years of vital importance to both the Roman and the Anglican Church; to say nothing of the interests touched by his prominent position in social and economic questions, that his biography was certain to be widely read and yield without doubt considerable profit. Readers of the two large volumes of the Biography will be surprised at the scantiness of acknowledgment.

There are many anecdotes scattered through the pages, and one or two dealing with this generosity of the Cardinal would have been welcome and illustrative.

Surprise will be closely allied to another feeling when it is known that, instead of having, as his story seems to imply, numerous conversations and lengthy intercourse with the only surviving sister of the Cardinal, Mrs. Austen, he in reality saw that lady *once only*, and for an hour or two. I will not touch upon the question of propriety, or rather of delicacy and honour, raised by the strange treatment of Manning by a writer to whom he had opened the treasures of his heart and memory. It will be enough for me to remark that, neither on this matter nor on the others, is Mr. Purcell worthy of confidence. To speak truly, I am happy to think that on this point and many others, Mr. Purcell's views will not be generally received either as final or complete, and that his statements will be found in many ways erroneous.

For the capacity of making errors is really phenomenal in Mr. Purcell. It may be said without exaggeration that he sometimes lights upon the truth by pure chance, and in spite of himself. He begins by voluntarily making a mistake of a year in the date of Manning's birth; in opposition to all previous testimony and existing documents. He makes a series of gross mistakes in his picture of the University of Oxford, which a glance at a Calendar would have saved him. He believes that the question of Catholic Emancipation, decided upon in 1829 by Sir R. Peel and Wellington, was still unsettled three years later. He confuses quite distinct periods, giving the name of Pusey to the Oxford Movement at a date when the Regius Professor of Hebrew had not publicly announced his sympathy with Tractarianism. I could multiply *ad infinitum* these proofs of an astounding ignorance and heedlessness.

Perhaps a plea of extenuating circumstances will be put forward for what concerns the Anglican period of Manning's life. After all, Mr. Purcell is a Catholic by birth, and though he ought to have prepared himself carefully to write of people and things that he did not know at first hand, indulgence may be shown him in this part.

But what can be said of the still more monstrous errors he makes when he has approached the Catholic period of the life of the Archbishop of

Westminster, and moves upon ground that ought to be familiar to him? Here I shall restrict myself to point out a single fault, but I think that, after having measured its extent, not many honest people will still be found to defend Mr. Purcell's competence.

Open the second volume of this monumental work at page 532. The very title of this nineteenth chapter will of itself be astonishing enough: *Second English Cardinal since the Reformation;* thus does our author entitle the section of his book in which he describes the promotion of Manning to the Roman scarlet. Thus, for him, the English cardinals who have received the hat since 1540, Pole, Allen, Weld, Norris, Howard, York, Acton, etc., have no reality, and before Manning, there was no other English prince of the Church but Wiseman!

Further, Mr. Purcell wonders that the claims of the great champion of infallibility at the Vatican Council could have been so long slighted. Had he been forgotten amongst the servants of Pius IX.? Had he aroused irreconcilable opposition in the Sacred College? Our historian accepts this latter hypothesis, and he writes the following lines, the flavour of which I should blame myself for spoiling by any comments whatsoever: "Pius IX. had not forgotten the Archbishop of Westminster. He had, from the first or the second year which followed the Council, proposed his name for election to the Sacred College. But the Cardinals, acting within the limits of their rights, had refused to elect him. Three years after the death of Cardinal Barnabo, Prefect of the Propaganda, who was not a friend of Manning's, the Pope again proposed the latter. It is the custom of the College of Cardinals to unanimously elect a candidate proposed for the second time, as they see in this act an expression of the deliberate will and determination of the Pope. In consequence, at the Consistory held on March 18, 1875, Archbishop Manning was admitted by a unanimous vote into the College of Cardinals."

Thus, Mr. Purcell, a Catholic historian, believes that the Sacred College is recruited by co-option, and the part played by the Sovereign Pontiff is limited to proposing candidates whom the cardinals reject or accept according to their will. Neither a very exact knowledge of history, nor a very strict method can be expected from a man who holds such views of the most important institutions of his own Church.

Nothing, indeed, equals the disorder, or rather the chaos, of Mr. Purcell's mind. Having to make use of a mass of original documents of various dates, coming from different sources, he ought, first, to have classified them, separating them into a series of contemporary papers, and into another, dealing with past events, and keeping chronological order; instead of this, he has, so to speak, flung them in the reader's face. Constantly a letter appears ten pages' distance after one that it should have preceded. Another appears three times, under three different dates, slightly changed in the text. He cuts into small fragments the papers of which he makes use, and scatters broadcast these *membra disjecta*. His own story is not less confused. He returns twice, thrice, even oftener, to the same subject, corrects himself, interrupts and contradicts himself, then forgets what he has just written.

NEED I say that it is not merely to give myself the satisfaction of protesting against this clumsy statement of a case that I have written these pages? Long ago, I confess, I sought the opportunity, whilst offering to the French public a short account of the history of the Oxford Movement, to render to Manning the enthusiastic homage that was in my heart. Brought at first to study him closely through the part he played in the great Dockers' Strike of 1889, I soon passed from his social to his charitable and religious activity, then to the consideration of his whole personality. How could one resist the powerful fascination of that noble episcopal figure, so rigid yet so modern, of such ascetic sanctity and such wide charity, of that old priest devoted, in the midst of a Protestant country and of the nineteenth century, to the ceaseless, uncompromising defence of the extremest views of the most militant Catholicism, and, at the same time, bending with boundless compassion over all the sufferings of his people?

Newman has great power over men's minds; Newman, that subtle logician who made dialectics supple to such a degree that he bestowed upon them the somewhat alarming characteristic of casuistry; that bold idealist, who was predestined to turn towards the Eternal realities the eyes of the inhabitants of a world in whose material reality he could never believe; that Christian sceptic for whom the postulates of the faith were the sole axioms of certainty, and who saw in the dogmas of revelation the only reply of God to the doubts and anguish of reason. Nothing would be more un-grateful than to wish to reject a master from whom our generation might learn so much. I know well what it has cost me to point out certain shadows in the brightness of that pure glory, that I might refute statements from which Manning would have suffered too cruelly. It required all the ingenuity of Mr. Purcell to re-kindle these past controversies. Thank Heaven! they cannot be perpetuated; those who have charitably applauded and used this myth of irreconcilable hostility between the two great restorers of English Catholicism, will not long rejoice.

These small differences have vanished in the presence of Death, in the majestic unity of eternal Christianity, and we can admire Manning without attacking Newman, or the reverse.

These retrospective controversies do not form the

attraction of our subject; that is to be found in this great venture of a soul. In this restless age, when so many vessels float aimlessly over the waters without compass, pilot, or rudder, there is nothing so consoling as the spectacle of a life which has dared the high seas and the tempest, has drawn near to many shores, and after despairing of a safe anchorage, has, after many dangers, entered port at last. There is, and will always be, an irresistible attraction in the story of those lives that have described vast parabola, that have known great sorrows, and made great sacrifices. The story of a Lamennais has passionately affected our contemporaries, beginning with faith, or at least with the steep will of a faith, imposed by main force on himself and others, and ending in the most grievous of shipwrecks, and in that sort of gloomy isolation of a Titan, crushed by the thunderbolt, able indeed to renounce Christ, but not to shake off his priest's robe. If that tragic story has so keenly interested us, shall we not find deep interest also in the striking contrast of the rise of a man's soul, led step by step, by the Spirit of Truth, from the rudimentary intuitions of faith to the summits of revealed religion and of supernatural certainties?

Contrasted with those noble, melancholy figures of a Lamennais, a Jouffroy, a Scherer, on whose brows a ray of grace seemed to rest, only to leave them the inconsolable regret of having for ever lost its brightness, it is well to see the figure, splendid in light and joy, of one of those whom God has led from the feeble beginnings of a still imperfect conversion to the glorious consummation of the work of their salvation. What if in Manning this development was not accomplished without a revolution, if he believed it to be his duty to quit the Church of his baptism, of his confirmation, and of his ordination, to ask from another Church freedom from the usurpations of the civil power, the unbroken preservation of the apostolic succession, organization of discipline, efficacy of the sacraments, and a real unity; if, born a Protestant, he, after twenty years of Anglican ministry, became a Catholic and a priest, all these things need not deprive him of our respect and sympathy. In these matters, I am sure, it is enough for a man to show himself to be honest, to secure our respect and sympathy, and Manning's honesty cannot be contested any more than his disinterestedness or his spirit of sacrifice.

Leaving, for the present, the examination of the validity of his motives on this solemn occasion, it is due to him to show, that the entire progress of this inner development from the day when the young clergyman's attention was called to the temporal function of the Holy Ghost, and to the promises of the presence of Jesus Christ, up to the hour when he believed that he found their perfect fulfilment in the authority of the Church and the infallibility of the Sovereign Pontiff, was far less a purely intellectual work than a work of the conscience. I venture to affirm, that whoever has read with an unprejudiced eye the documents, that is, the letters and fragments of his private diary during the decisive phase from 1847 until 1851, whatever may be his views about these matters, even though he may see a signal and fatal error in Manning's gradual approach to Catholicism, must yet recognize and acknowledge the sincerity of his efforts, the uprightness of his intentions, the growth of his piety.

At first sight, this statement or this avowal might seem a dilettante's *jeu d'esprit*, or even a lesson in scepticism. Yet who will assert that God has promised the privilege of infallibility on all points, as a reward for holiness, to the individual soul? In writing a man's history, prejudices, theories, doctrines themselves, matter little ; the life itself, the acts, words, thoughts, must be grasped and reproduced. I should have strangely falsified Manning's portrait, if I had not shown, heedless of the varying inferences that might be drawn from it, the perfect sincerity of his spiritual *crisis*, the predominance in his thought of the great, essential principles, the facts of Christianity, his ardent concern for the unique question of salvation, and his comparative indifference to a

mass of secondary problems, which to some minds
contain the necessary points of departure for all
Catholicizing development. Here is, in any case,
a man of whom it cannot be said, that if he abjured
Protestantism, he did so lightly : he struggled for
six years against himself; neither did he abjure it
from a liking for ceremonial and pomp of worship :
his parish church, when he left it, was like St.
Mary's at Oxford under Newman, Evangelical in
its simplicity and severity; even when he had
become a Catholic, he never gave to external rites
the disproportionate importance that is given to
them by Anglican Ritualists. Neither did he
abjure Protestantism from disdain of the Bible : to
the end of his life he made a daily, close study of
it. Nor was it through ambition : an Archdeacon
at the age of thirty-two, he received at thirty-six
the offer of a post that would have opened to him
almost the highest dignities; he was morally sure
of the English episcopate, while in Catholicism
(then singularly despised and disliked by the
English people) he was a mere recruit and novice.
Everything concurs to justify the view that I feel
bound to take of this conversion, and to show in
it a most important act of obedience and faith.
This fact is important, essential, not only for the
right estimate of Manning's personality, but also
when we consider the value of those ideas whose
chief representative the Archbishop of Westminster

became in the second part of his career. If it is essential to recognize that the Catholicism and the Ultramontanism of Manning were the results of a spiritual development, it is still more so to ascertain that it was the same work of conscience that brought forth the social conceptions of the Cardinal.

On opposite sides, two schools or two parties are bent on representing Catholicism or social Christianity as a sort of purely lay and earthly doctrine, stripped of all supernatural elements, entirely devoted to the solution of a painful problem by means of human activity. Those who will not accept social Christianity, because they hate Christ's religion, and those who will not accept Christian Socialism because they hate the mere thought of an organic reform of society, agree with certain men of more pronounced zeal, but ignorant in their good will, in order to deprive this great movement of its true sense and import. To bring down religion to an earthly level; to efface, or at least put in the background, all supernatural elements of Christianity; to treat dogma as old-fashioned rubbish, which is preserved through a sort of pious weakness for the past; to make human solidarity the alpha and omega of morality, without resting it on the fatherhood of God revealed by the brotherhood of Christ; to transform the Church into an immense Friendly or

Benefit Society; to wish to perform the miracle of human love in the sphere of men's interests, after having rejected the miracle of divine love on the Cross; in a word, to pretend to renew humanity, to establish the reign of justice and charity on the earth without the help of those great deeds which contain all salvation, the salvation of the species as that of the individual, such is the vague, unhealthy dream of minds who think they can kill two birds with one stone, unchristianize the Church, and with it regenerate the world. They would not all define with this pitiless precision the object of their secret desires or their unconscious aspirations. There are souls still half-religious, but tainted by the deadly contagion of modern rationalism, who think that all that lessens the share of dogma and increases that of practical activity in the Church makes her truer to her vocation, and more conformable to her Master's design. It is often the noble error of ardent and generous hearts touched profoundly by the sufferings and the injustice of society, indignant at the indifference, I had almost said the passive complicity of the Church, who long to see her fulfil her sacred mission, and who lose sight of the fact that without these dogmas, in which, they say, she is selfishly absorbed, she would have neither authority, nor strength, nor means of action, nor motive power. In our day, when it is so difficult to maintain resolutely our testimony in honour of Christian supernaturalism and of Jesus Christ, the miracle of miracles, nothing is so dangerous as the coalition of very practical rationalism and imprudent charity. Therefore one cannot profess enough gratitude for the inflexible champions of principles, who, while being the first to preach with incomparable ardour the social crusade of the Church, have been careful to connect this crusade closely with the profession of objective, dogmatic, orthodox Christianity. They have not merely washed the Church from a reproach; they have offered to the world the only efficacious instrument of salvation.

What particular value would men ever attach to the purely natural, human, and terrestrial action of a great corporate body? Without a divine mandate, without the help of her Master, without the Gospel to awaken consciences, without the sacraments to nourish souls, what could the Church be, do, even hope for in social matters? Social Christianity will either be Christian in the full sense of the word, or it will not exist. That is what Manning set forth, with incomparable strength and clearness, not only in all he said and wrote on social Catholicism in the last years of his life, but by his whole career. He believed he ought to become a Catholic, because he did not believe he could otherwise remain a Christian;

in virtue of the same need, he was a Catholic upholding authority and centralization; finally, he was the initiator of social Christianity or Catholicism through his very fidelity to doctrinal Catholicism. All this development is alike connected and self-complete. It is one of the greatest honours to the memory of Manning to have been the first representative—at least in his country—of the beneficent doctrine which the social Encyclicals of Leo XIII. have since sanctioned and set forth, and which has the double object of reminding the Church of the performance of an essential part of her divine vocation, and of offering to our unhealthy society the remedy of supernatural Christianity.

III

THERE remains to be considered the question of principle which has been urged upon me with so much persistency from several sides. I should much have preferred not to have to discourse to the reader of things which belong to the domain of conscience, and about which a discreet reserve seems most fitting. Nevertheless, there are subjects which cannot be treated in a certain way without pledging oneself, at least implicitly, to follow out one's thought to the end, and this I should fail to do, were I to be silent to any who ask me, in the name of what I have already said, to say still more. They have easily distinguished in my articles a lively sympathy, not only for the man whose life I have sketched, but for some of the principles whose representative he was. They have laid me under the necessity of clearly stating my position with regard to the question of Catholicism. If it were only a matter of the indelicate curiosity which scents out with delight

45

any piece of scandal, or even of that pitiless logic which will, at all costs, show you the extreme consequences of your own statements, nobody, I am sure, would blame me for keeping to the impersonal expression of my thought. I am told that I have pained certain minds, wounded certain consciences; I must, therefore, try to reply as frankly as possible to these statements, and explain myself as clearly as I can upon the state of mind that has caused these anxieties.

First, I gladly acknowledge the pleasure I have felt, not only in drawing the portrait of a great Christian, but in rendering homage to a great Catholic. Setting aside all question of allegiance to any confession of faith, and assuming that the spirit of the Reformation should be free from all sectarian prejudice, ever ready to rise above divergencies of forms and secondary differences, in order to seize points of similitude and to greet the living unity of the invisible Church, it seemed to me *à priori* that one of the best means of showing my respect for that spirit, was to sketch freely, but with a loving hand, the portrait of such a man as Manning.

This method of practically proving the breadth of view of certain doctrinaires of religious Liberalism has not proved a success. In general, the Cardinal, the Ultramontane, the fugitive from Protestantism, has not been pardoned for the sake

46

of the friend of the poor, the ascetic, the imitator of Christ. They have not even seemed to understand the proper duty of an historian, how, when he wishes to bring a man vividly before his readers, he must penetrate into the farthest recesses of his mind, discover his most secret impulses, share his feelings, make his affections his own, see with his eyes, speak through his mouth, in short, assume his personality.

I no longer remember which of my critics bantered me about this expression *hero of charity*, which I had applied to Manning. He noted that the Cardinal, an octogenarian, died in his bed,— and then he began to jeer. For my part, I was unaware until then that a man must die young and of a violent death to deserve that title, and I had thought that we said " heroic charity," as we say "heroic honesty, heroic justice," to express a certain supernatural degree of virtue, to which man cannot rise without the help of grace. In any case, this is my confession, and if, to profess deep admiration for a man whose life one proposes to write, is to lay oneself open to an accusation of clear partiality, I have deserved that verdict. But this is not all. Bound, above all, to study the development of Manning's mind just as it showed itself, to follow its bent, to see things from the same standpoint as he did, I thought I ought to accept the same data of the problem that offered

itself to him. I have generalized as little as possible. The great suit between Protestantism and
Catholicism, for instance, was, as far as he was
concerned, fought out on the rather narrow and
artificial ground of Anglicanism. He had to
choose, not between the religion of authority and
the religion of liberty, but between the religion of
authentic, legitimate, and real authority and the
religion of factitious and illusory authority. He
was perfectly conscious of this circumstance, which
modified to a certain extent the validity of his
conclusions. At the moment of taking the decided
step, and of performing the irrevocable act that
was to turn him from an Anglican into a Catholic,
he felt so strongly that it was not Protestantism
per se whose insufficiency he had proved, that he
admitted the possibility of resorting to the mystic
idealism of the Invisible Church, *i. e.* to the true
conception of the Reformation, quite as much as
to the objective realism of Rome. He rejected
only one course, a return to the pseudo-Catholicism
of the Anglican Church.

This must be borne in mind in reading these
pages. To Manning's mind, under a naturally
rather confused and imperfect form,—to the mind
of the writer of these lines, under a much clearer
form,—most of the difficulties, objections, criticisms,
reproaches, grievances, which ended by leading the
Archdeacon of Chichester to Rome, arose, not from

that rather metaphysical entity, Protestantism in itself, but from that very real, very peculiar institution, the Church of England.

Therefore it would be unjust merely to separate from their context, and apply unceremoniously to Protestantism itself, arguments or imputations that concern that very individual form of religion, Anglicanism. It is even very startling to see some vehement champions of Protestantism, in their ignorant zeal, take under their protection an ecclesiastical Establishment that positively does not claim part or lot in their principles, and repudiates all connection with them. I refer here to a very fine passage in the first Pastoral Letter of Manning, Archbishop of Westminster, on the attitude of the Church towards the Dissenters : that, to his mind, the Anglican Church would most probably show itself, in the name of the Anglo-Catholic pretensions, far more aggressive and unjust towards Protestant Nonconformity, than would Catholicism. This told, I should seriously fail in fidelity to a higher truth, if I did not directly add that, as an historian, I should have had far more difficulty in identifying myself with my hero, or in reproducing in their full force those arguments which, whilst aimed at Anglicanism, do, in a measure, attack Protestantism, if I had not felt a deep sympathy with the very groundwork of Manning's ideas.

I know not whether I shall succeed—I do not say,

in making my readers share—but in making them comprehend the state of mind that dictated to me and that justifies, in my eyes, my attitude to these questions : for I believe myself to have been both authorized and obliged to write all I have written—not omitting a single word—yet at the same time to do only what I have done, without going a step farther.

To form the conception that if there is a Church —in the Catholic sense of the word—there is only one, and that it is the Church whose centre is Rome; to profess that, if Christianity is not merely the religion of pure and simple individualism; if, outside the mystical communion of the soul with its Saviour, there is unity and the common life of the members of the body of Christ, the Christian organism implies the decisive part played by tradition and authority; to believe that if the promised help, the presence of the Holy Spirit bears not only on the personal assurance of salvation, the providential preservation of the sacred trust of the Faith demands fully an objective mechanism; to see in the sacraments powerful realities, incomparable means of grace and life, if they are not merely the mnemotechnic signs of the great facts of Redemption; to understand that since reason is not the final court of appeal in matters of faith, it must disown the principle of free inquiry and acknowledge the sovereignty of another judge; these are opinions that will perhaps scandalize many Protestants without fully satisfying Catholics. This is not all; at the time that my mind was opened to the somewhat hypothetical intuition of the living unity of the Catholic system, experience revealed to me the practical consequences of some Protestant premisses. I may be allowed here to remark that I approach this subject with some emotion. Two years ago, speaking on a similar subject to a strictly Protestant audience in a very Protestant town which I had intentionally chosen, I declared that, rather than utter certain words and expose myself to certain interpretations in a centre where the atmosphere would be essentially different and saturated with quite other elements, I would prefer to keep silence. If I now break it, it is because I am compelled to do so, and I believe I cannot touch better upon these delicate questions than by describing with all honesty the progress of my thought.

The whole of Protestantism, especially in countries where French is spoken, has been for some time on the eve of a terrible crisis. Theology is about to communicate not only to the clergy, but to the whole of the faithful, the principal results of its great works in criticism and speculation. To-day the watch-word is—" No more esoterics ; no more dualism, either more or less conscious or avowed between what is elaborated in the study and what is preached from the pulpits. Frankness,

frankness, above all, frankness!" Need I say how much this movement seems to me legitimate, or rather imperative. We should calumniate our fathers, the men of those generations who garnered in and transmitted to us the inheritance of faith and of zeal from the *Revival*, were we to ascribe to them in any degree the intention of keeping the laity apart or sheltered from the results of theological culture. There was neither plot nor conspiracy, nor even a settled plan. This sort of dualism was produced because, in fact, most of the leaders were themselves still in the trammels of former ideas, and would have been much puzzled to have to communicate to their flocks unverified hypotheses with insufficient foundation, and systems still merely in a conjectural state. Nevertheless, long since, one of the ideas on which the generation of the *Revival* believed itself bound to base the edifice of its faith, the idea of theopneusty, or plenary inspiration of the Scriptures, received a decided shock. I think that, at the present time, there would be found few of the avowed orthodox who would not heartily accept (at least in its groundwork) Edmond Scherer's famous pamphlet, so violently denounced in 1848. But this was only a beginning. It is not enough to destroy the simple confidence that sees in each book, each page, each line, each word of the Bible, a direct and authentic revelation, a communication straight from God. The souls of the

52

simple, astonished, terrified at this great void, must be shown what will replace the authority of the Bible. And everywhere, on all points, this double work goes on; on the one hand, by finishing the overthrow of the erroneous conceptions of the past; on the other, by substituting for them notions more conformable with the present criterions of theological truth, capable at the same time of offering, as formerly, a support to individual and collective religious life. One cannot be much surprised that these two parts of the work do not make equal progress.

Demolition always goes on more rapidly than reconstruction. It is easier to explode the theopneustical hypothesis, to destroy the unity, authenticity, and antiquity of the Pentateuch, to bring back the whole history of Israel to the Period of the Kings as a point of departure, and to the so-called post-exilic texts, as documents with a date, than to reconstruct an acceptable, and, above all, a livable theory of the authority of the Bible and the nature of the Old Covenant.

It must be remembered that, historically, Protestantism has lived on a double principle; one, called *formal*, the authority of the Scriptures; the other, *material*, Justification by Faith. These two principles are strictly interdependent. The first affirms that Jesus Christ is the sole source of man's knowledge of salvation, that every soul receives directly

53

and personally the light necessary to collect the
message of God from the documents of the history
of Redemption ; the second, that Jesus Christ alone
is the source of salvation, that it suffices for every
soul to come into direct and immediate contact
with the Saviour, apart from all external means of
grace, for it to receive the fulness of Redemption.
It is evident that the former of these fundamental
axioms of the Reformation, viz. Jesus Christ, sole
and sufficient source of the knowledge of salvation
through the Scriptures, without tradition and without interpreter—is, if not absolutely imperilled, at
least thrown into strange difficulties, by the progress of criticism. Formerly, it seemed very easy
to the most ignorant, the humblest believer to listen
to the voice of God, which alone, in its written form,
he was bound to obey, as his own conscience. He
took his Bible, turned over the pages, and believed
each word to be a Divine message. Now, he must
ask himself : " Is this passage, this word, really
authentic ? Am I reading Christ's very words, or
are they St. John's imagination ? Am I consulting
an account given by an eye-witness, or is it not some
tendencious result of the transactions of Judæo-
Christian diplomacy ? " I know what will be the
answer: the inner sense, the experience of the
Christian, suffices to discern his Master's voice. But
even this principle has its limits, under pain of falling into absolute subjection to the sole sovereignty

of the *testimonium spiritus*.   Faith demands something objective, something to grasp ; the conscience is not satisfied unless it finds something truly greater than itself, something which it cannot infallibly judge.

I believe that the Reformers would have little relished, in their robust good sense and need of what is practical, these subtle theories, where, under pretext of carrying to its extreme limits the second of their formulas—Jesus, the only source of salvation, and, consequently, reducing to a minimum the importance of the accessory elements, and, if one may dare say so, of the outer covering of this great fact of Redemption,—people hold cheap the authority of Scripture, that authority to which, for their part, they attached no less value than to the first of their formulas, and in which they saw the means whereby Christ willed to secure the objective knowledge of His work.   Such a work of destruction cannot be stopped at pleasure;   when the authority of Scripture is destroyed, the person of the Saviour will not be long untouched.   Those who aim, with the greatest sincerity, I feel sure, at cracking the shell, the better to enjoy its kernel, at breaking the vase, the more fully to breathe its perfume, will confess sooner or later that they have pursued a dangerous chimera.

This famous theological renovation affects all points at once;   it extends to all domains.   It touches dogmatism, for example, when it demonstrates to us that there are no dogmas in the Gospel; that dogma is purely and simply the subjective and intellectual expression of a given state of the soul; that evolution, in the strict Darwinian sense of the word, presides over the formation of dogmas, that religion in a final analysis is reduced, according to the acute, deep saying of Matthew Arnold, to "morality touched by emotion." Now it is a theory of knowledge that we are required to accept as the preliminary condition of all religious speculations and that declares all opinion to be relative, any affirmation bearing on the essence, or any objective concept, to be radically impossible. Then comes a theology which declares, first of all, that God is only and could be only the complete expression of the ideas relating to the Divinity that may be found in men's minds taken as a whole; the Ego, moreover, is only a conscious sequel of localized sensations affirming implicitly their interdependence; that, finally, the true restoration of Christianity, *i. e.* of the power of life and of salvation which humanity cannot do without, implies previously received acceptance of the hyper-Kantian criticism, or rather of the scepticism of Hume, and the formal repudiation of realism in every domain. Ritschl is the prophet of this new dispensation, as Schleiermacher was of an anterior phase; and with Hegel, Kant and Hume, followed by Darwin, must serve as masters to this authentic

interpretation of Christian revelation that we have
at last obtained. Certainly I do not assert that
these doctrines are already accepted in every
Protestant pulpit, but are they not often the sub-
stance of the teaching given to future members of
the clergy? are they not floating in the air? Does
one not hear, and it is indeed a characteristic sign,
Laodiceans, full of good intentions, declare that,
after all, there is much that is good and true in
these ideas; that dogma has always clouded the
religious atmosphere and made it heavy; that the
living and sacred person of the Saviour will shine
more fully, and be in more intimate and direct
communion with us, when the shadow of dogma
has passed from before it? Is there no talk of the
need for reconciliation with the representatives of
that theology that calls itself Liberal, and which was
energetically opposed and eliminated as much as
possible from the bosom of the Church by the last
generation? Is not the air full of the sound of
those short-lived reconciliations which must, we are
assured, put an end to the scandal of antagonism
between the sons of the Huguenots, but only by
substituting a graver scandal, that of a cordial
understanding between Christians and philo-
sophers, believers and freethinkers, in the same
Church?

The fundamental tendency is to anti-dogmatism,
to a religion where dogma will play, if any, a very

minor part, and where at the same time what might
have remained of the idea of a Church, of a
conception of the means of grace and of the sacraments, will completely disappear. I certainly have
not the melancholy pretension of considering this
to be the universal state of things; I merely note
tendencies. Thank God! every one knows that
even under the most perverted and imperfect forms,
there remains enough religious life to feed powerful
currents. Who could be so much blinded by party
or sectarian spirit as not to declare joyfully that, in
the Reformed Churches as in the Catholic Church,
there are saintly lives, triumphant deaths, splendid
examples of the mighty power of grace, and that
the one incontestable apostolic succession, that
which secures to Christ and to humanity an unbroken line of zealous, faithful servants, works
nevertheless, outside the narrow limits of an historical communion? Any one who allowed himself
to pass wholesale condemnation on the men whose
shoes' latchet, in all probability, he is not worthy to
unloose, would be rightly bound to account for
such severity.

Such is not, I venture to believe, the feeling I
now obey. Is it really imagined that filial piety
vanishes so rapidly, and that it is so easy to fail in
respect to the memory of those to whom a man
owes everything, not only religion, but conscience
and honour? Is it then so presumptuous, while

feeling the sincerest gratitude, the tenderest veneration for the memories dear to us, to avow, that the
faith that proved sufficient for a soul nearer to God
and less under the power of evil, has been found
insufficient for oneself? I am truly astonished that
people will not see that there may be real humility
in the anxiety of a conscience that cannot be satisfied for its own salvation with a doctrine which no
doubt afforded the fullest and firmest satisfaction to
the needs of those whom it most loves and respects.
A perfectly upright, pure soul (one of those natures,
in which, as was said with happy audacity by the
great Christian philosopher, Charles Secrétan, original sin is reduced to the smallest amount) is
freed in a measure from the conditions that call
forth a series of urgent needs in an average nature.
Such a soul can discover vital elements, feed upon
them and prosper in an atmosphere where one less
happily gifted will be choked and withered. There
are consciences which have only to catch a lightning
glimpse of the Saviour's Divine face to be brought
into direct communion with Him. Their rapid and
certain flight needs no well-swept paths, no ladders
or solid stairs, such as are required in their progress
by the heavier, slower, and more human steps of less
privileged beings. A sort of pre-established harmony between the Master and some disciples allows
them to hear and recognize His voice with certainty ;
they have no need for anxiety about the external

signs and infallible marks which the mass of the flock cannot do without.

I think that to confess humbly that one is bound to follow the King's highway, is hardly to exalt oneself as a judge of those whom God has allowed to walk in the bye-paths. If, for some choice spirits, grace is in a measure independent of dogma, it does not follow that for everybody dogma can be safely laid aside, nor that to claim for oneself the firm support of dogma is to contest the grace of other and happier souls. God grants to some the miracle of individual salvation that works by strange ways.

If it has been justly and forcibly said that some atheists make one believe in God, and have too many virtues not to be Christians, in fact, how much the more ought one to say that there are men whom the imperfections of their Church and their theology cannot deprive of the one thing needful ? To count upon this exceptional treatment for oneself would be to tempt God; to seek for oneself in all sincerity the ordinary conditions of grace is by no means to pass judgment upon those privileged souls. It is rather proclaiming one's own weakness, to confess that one is more liable to the harmful effects of an unhealthy atmosphere; that unsupported and unhelped by tradition and author-ity, one's faith gives way, that if dogma grows dim to one's eyes, grace suffers; that the results of modern theology or the unrestrained exercise of the critical faculty or of free inquiry, if not met by a corrective and needful counterpoise, will shake to its foundations the work of Redemption in one's soul. I perfectly comprehend that denunciations, even ridicule, should be called forth by this strange weakness of mind, this feebleness of will; but I positively deny the right of any one to throw moral censure on this attitude, and loftily to condemn in it an indefinable want of respect for those who practised individual religion to the end, and who bequeathed to their children a purely Protestant name. This argument comes with peculiarly bad grace from those who have made a sort of intellectual dogma of free inquiry, who admit no exception from the supreme jurisdiction of criticism, and who, apparently, are not opposed to the Reformers' exercise of the right to revise tradition and to revoke the conclusions of those very men from whom they had received the sacred trust of the Faith. If the Reformation could legitimately re-ascend the stream of time and strike off the twelve or thirteen centuries of Catholic development, because of the consequences, fatal in its eyes, of the principle of authority, there should be no outcry against those who are anxious as to the consequences of the individualistic principle, and who desire to re-ascend the stream and to grasp again the living unity of Christianity.

Amongst those who still take their ground on the supernatural element in religion, *i.e.* the Incarnation of the Son of God and Redemption through the Cross, who is there who does not feel alarmed by the more or less insidious progress of the tendency to shake the authority of the Scriptures, and to reduce the Christ of the Expiation and of the Justification to the dimensions of a mere mortal, incomparable though he may be? Who has not sometimes sorrowfully asked himself, if, after all, it is not the legitimate use of the methods honoured by the Reformers that has finished by striking a deadly blow at the dogmas, or rather at the fundamental facts of the religion of salvation? There are hours when the greatest optimist questions himself upon the solidity of a Church that rests upon Justification by Faith and upon the inspiration and authority of the Scriptures, yet sees these two foundations beaten down by the very weapons that she thought to use in their defence, for the schism of the sixteenth century was the will of God, and restored truths forgotten or effaced by Catholicism. His position is a sad one when, at times, it seems as if he must choose between the very principles and the objects of the Reformation, between the method which it inaugurated as the only fitting one in matters of faith and the realization of the ideal of the Christian life set forth by it.

It is plain that you have not to deal here with a vague Romantic reaction, as some dishonest critics would have us believe, a St. Martin's summer of Neo-Catholicism, in the manner of Chateaubriand, *i. e.* a craving for æsthetic emotions.

Rightly or wrongly, it is the very essence of Christianity that is at stake, and one asks from many sides, whether Christian supernaturalism is not, indeed, more safe in a Church professing to possess full means of grace, in a religious community over which the ages have passed, and which claims or offers the triple guarantee of unity, authority, and perpetuity in apostolic succession, in the supremacy of the Holy See, in all its hierarchical organization, in all the objective realities of its worship. One cannot help feeling some uneasiness when one sees the Anglo-Catholic movement come, not only to the abjuration of its chief initiators, but to the transformation of Anglicanism, when one watches the efforts that that great Church makes (separated for three hundred years from the centre of Roman unity) in order to regain possession of the advantages of the Catholic system, yet without coming to any act of submission; when one sees her claim apostolic succession for her bishops, validity of ordination for her clergy, when she restores the Eucharistic service, even the sacrifice of the Mass, when she establishes Confession and the Sacrament of Penance, tries to reconstitute religious orders; in short, borrows from the Papal Church all that gives strength to the latter, yet will not pay the price. It is thus that Catholicism takes its revenge,—a revenge, without doubt, against an ecclesiastical establishment that has always borne in its constitution the germ of all the contradictions of the politicians its founders, always suffering from the effect of their contradictory interests; but also a revenge, taken in the very midst of the classic land of individualistic Protestantism, on the morrow of that splendid Evangelical Revival, in presence of those Nonconformist Churches that are filled with the spirit of the Reformation. And this is not all: our generation sees arise before it, with ever-increasing imperiousness, a mass of questions in which the very principle of individualism seems maimed from the outset.

Is it indeed the Christianity of the Reformation that will be able to play the part of spiritual leaven in this great social change that we all foresee, of which certain symptoms already make themselves felt, a change that must take place at any cost, if our social systems want to avoid a revolution, and if they truly exist for the sake of justice? Will it in time give birth, not only to such men as Charles Secrétan, to the thinkers that set the problem and study it under every aspect, but to men like Manning and Gibbons, deputies of the Church, where there is poverty to be relieved or charity to organize?

I know well that Protestantism has had its Shaftesbury; but will there ever be found again the
miracle of a truly divine largeness of heart with an
unequalled narrowness of thought, that alliance or
alloy of heroic charity with a kind of morbid
shrinking of the mind? Even if it were to be met
with again, would it suffice for our time? Lastly,
is there not in the present time, by the side of
a thirst for pleasure and dilettanteism, a need for
renunciation, for asceticism, discipline, obedience,
holy and secluded living, regulated and cloistered
activity and contemplation, a need such as is always felt in times of decadence and dissolution, or
of moral and social decay, when these have still
within them a germ of life and resurrection, as for
instance in the fourth and fifth centuries of our
era? These are needs, not perhaps incompatible
with the very spirit of the Reformation, but which
can scarcely now find organized and regular satisfaction outside Catholicism.

Monastic life has its place in the Catholic system;
I do not know whether one could be found for it,
even if it were modified on essential points, in the
Protestant system. And as to those mystical
needs of more intimate union, more complete pene-
tration of the soul, more direct, and at the same
time more objective, possession of Christ, are not
the sacraments, such as the Catholic Church adores
and administers, fitter to quench a thirst than

the mere commemorations to which Protestantism
—at least that outside the Lutheran Church—has
too often reduced the most solemn acts of the
religious life?

While fully acknowledging the austere grandeur
sometimes offered by the Reformed worship, when it
does not ape from afar the externals of Catholic
ceremonies, and when the imagination can retrace the
historical causes of this simplicity, I may be allowed
to say that the need for a thorough renovation is felt
in every part of Protestantism. A form of worship
offering the daily repetition of the great drama of
expiation, with the ever-renewed symbols of the one
Sacrifice on the Cross, with the majestic accents
of a liturgy that goes far back to primitive Christianity, that continually asserts the Communion of
Saints and the perfect unity of the Church of Christ,
all this seems more fitted to attract and retain souls,
weary of the subtleties of analysis, the dry statements of reason, and the sophisms of doubt. I do
not think I am alone in feeling this, and in feeling
it deeply; yet it is certain that, while sometimes
conscious of a kind of intellectual and moral
haunting, while sometimes asking ourselves whether
we are not resisting our consciences, we do not
feel able so far, either to shake off a painful uncertainty, or make up our minds to take one of
those irrevocable steps that are justifiable only
when they are inevitable.

Doubtless, it is good to believe that at a certain height the most diverging lines meet; that there is a level where men like St. Augustine, St. Vincent de Paul, Pascal, and Manning are bathed in the same rays of light and glory and sing the same songs of triumph as men like Luther, Coligny, Franke, Vinet, and Shaftesbury. It is sweet to remember with what supreme largeness of heart, some great Christians have delighted in forgetting their secondary differences of opinion, and proclaiming their agreement on fundamental points of faith, such as that venerable priest of the diocese of Paris who was eager to associate the prayers of his friend, a Protestant clergyman, with his sacerdotal jubilee. All this gratifies the heart, but we must not indulge in too convenient fictions, or take refuge in a sort of cloudy idealism. We have just witnessed the failure of one of those premature attempts in which the desire for conciliation prevails over the search for conditions of agreement; when one says—"Peace, peace," where there is no peace; attempts that end, in spite of the best intentions, in complete discord.

On February 14, 1895, Lord Halifax told the members of the English Church Union at Bristol—"Union with Rome is desirable, it is possible." He expressed the wish to see the Roman Church make overtures to the English Church which would bring about a bodily reunion. The letter of Leo

XIII. *ad Anglos* was in a measure the reply of the Sovereign Pontiff to this request, and one might have heard in it the voice of a father. Ardent souls formed the hope of a prompt return of the Anglican Church to Roman unity. They entertained strong illusions, fed themselves on chimeras until the Encyclical *Satis cognotum* formulated the necessary conditions of any reconciliation, and re-iterated with the authority of the successor of St. Peter the lesson that Manning had already given in his Pastoral Letter of 1866 to the mediators who wished for compromise. Between Catholicism, even when it is represented by a Leo XIII., and Protestantism, even when it has reduced to a minimum its profession of the principles of the Reformation, and tries, like the Anglicanism of Lord Halifax, to follow a *via media*, equally distant from Rome and Geneva, there is scarcely any possible compromise; it seems to be a case of submission or combat. This is the confession that one is sometimes reduced to make to oneself, after having indulged in the sincerest dreams of factitious reconciliations or unnatural alliances. Vain illusions!

The Reformed and the Catholic Churches have no doubt in common what constitutes the trust of Revelation and of Faith, eternal Christianity; but under what different—or rather contrary—forms is this common foundation hidden! To speak the truth, there is no midway halting-place between the two creeds. One must make a deliberate, conscious choice between one or the other. If ever this sad alternative is imposed on any among us, may God preserve him from ever forgetting what he owes to the religion of his fathers! It is to them, it is often to his own father that a son owes the little Christianity which gives him life. There lies for some, the private drama roughly made use of by controversialists who see in it only matter for dispute. May it not be sometimes, in order to be faithful to the spirit, to the lessons, to the principles of those to whom one owes the knowledge of salvation, that one is tempted to be unfaithful to their doctrine?

Guilt would lie in acting heedlessly, in listening to other accents than those of the conscience, in being false to the memories of those great effects of grace that have shown themselves brilliantly in the communion in which one was born, in repudiating the memory of those generous, chivalrous, faithful, and pure lives, vowed to the service of God and man, of those still more glorious deaths in which the power of the Divine life was manifested with incomparable force. If one's heart is in the right place, one runs little risk of not giving due weight to these considerations; but it would not be less guilty to stop one's ears with sentimental reminiscences and to refuse to listen to the imperious appeal of conscience, if ever she says—" The work of destruction goes on; for others it is perhaps without danger, but not for you; Christian super-naturalism, the dogmas of Scripture, vanish under the knife of searching criticism; the object of faith, all objective religion, is reduced to a nebulous con-dition; theology gives us a Bible, the disjointed pieces of which require to be printed in various colours, and which the learned, only after much research, can read with discernment; it offers us an impalpable, intangible Christ, a sort of twilight ghost, fallen at the same time from His divinity and His humanity, without historical reality in the past, or celestial reality in the present, or super-natural reality in the Sacraments." The cup offered to us is full of a deadly drink: let us reject this poison! Like the woman of Scripture, rather than let Christ escape, this generation will perhaps have to seize the hem of His garment. Perhaps, even, it will have to follow closely in the footsteps of His disciples, though it may be only to pass under that shadow of Peter that cured the sick at Jerusalem.

PROTESTANT YEARS

(1833—1851)

I

FOUR years ago, separated only by a few months, two men died in England laden with years and labours, two Cardinals of the Holy Roman Church, two of the men who, in this faithless age and in a country apart from the centre of unity since the Reformation, have the most contributed to restore Catholicism to honour, and to give back to it the prestige and the authority of one of the greatest spiritual powers of our day. One of these two men passed away through the exhaustion of extreme old age in a monastic house in a suburb of Birmingham. His simple coffin received the homage of the highest English intellects, proud to salute in John Henry Newman one of the masters of that bold method of apologetics, that subtle psychology and that fearless dialectic whose imperishable model has, to a certain extent, been given by Pascal, and which overcomes reason

71

under a seeming scepticism, only to place it at the foot of the Cross. The other, younger, but worn out by the fatigue of ceaseless activity and by the practice of rigorous asceticism, breathed his last sigh in that simple house at Westminster where he had chosen to establish his archiepiscopal residence. He expired almost at the same hour as the young Duke of Clarence, and it might have been thought that in a nation deeply loyal and monarchical, and moreover Protestant in name and tradition, the regrets excited by the premature end of the heir presumptive to the throne might have scarcely left any room for sorrow over the octogenarian, the fugitive from Anglicanism, the head of English Catholicism. Nevertheless, his funeral had the imposing, sublime, unique characteristics of a great, popular demonstration. For a whole people—the workers, the poor, the suffering—arose to mourn a hero of charity.

It was a sight hardly to be expected in the England of the last decade of the nineteenth century. No one had chastised proud reason like the first of these princes of a Church whose communion had been rejected by England for three hundred and fifty years; no one like him had treated practical materialism in such a scathing fashion; no one had disdained or rather ignored those boasted stages of progress, those famous mechanical inventions, those pretended conquests of science, the foolish admiration for which forms almost all the religion of many of our contemporaries. No one like Cardinal Manning had scandalized that Anglicanism whose former hope and support he had been, that average Liberalism that sees no enemy except the Church, no freedom except in oppressing consciences, that affectedly grave clericalism from which he had freed himself by the very power of his religious and ecclesiastical opinions, that accepted political economy whose commonplaces are so convenient for the selfishness of certain classes, and whose laws and principles he had often seemed to take pleasure in violating and contesting. And more than that. Both these renovators of Catholicism had issued from Protestantism wounding it as they departed. The first half of the life of both had been given to the service of the English Church in the ranks of her clergy. Both, though in very different degrees, had been party-leaders; both had fought for the Church of their fathers against Rome and her claims. They had rescued souls on the verge of desertion and submission to the authority of the Vicar of Jesus Christ. One of them had inaugurated and directed for twelve years that great Anglo-Catholic movement whose command, for a time, had passed to the other from the faithless hands of its general when he went over to the enemy in 1845. At their bidding, that great current broke forth whose waters finally threw them in spite of themselves on the opposite shore, but not before they had fertilized the rather barren and ungrateful soil of Anglicanism, and induced it to bring forth a whole harvest of piety, spiritual life, and charitable works.

By one of those impulses that defy calculation and bring reason to confusion, England, Protestant, Anglican, and especially Antipapist, has celebrated and honoured in these two men, two of the greatest enemies of those compromises that are as dear to her in religion as in politics, two revolutionaries, resolved to overthrow, in the name of absolutism, that rule of the ecclesiastical mean between the two extremes to which she is so much attached. The history of these two lives can alone explain this seeming paradox. These biographies, with those of Pusey and of some other persons of secondary importance, give the whole history of Anglo-Catholicism.

I make no claim to write it here. To-day, I can give a rapid sketch only of a subject which, like the Jansenism of the seventeenth century, would require, to treat it as it deserves, the conscientious erudition, the delicate psychology, the incomparable method of Sainte-Beuve in his *Port Royal.*

This movement has produced, I venture to say, in English religion and society, a revolution no less extensive nor less deep than that political change effected at the same time by the Great Reform

Bill. It was initiated by a few members of the University and parish clergy, having for its headquarters the Common Room of the Fellows of Oriel College, Oxford, and for its leader, a young, unknown clergyman, unconscious of his own genius, and scarcely loosed from the narrow bonds of Evangelical Protestantism. It is radically impossible, without a fairly exact view of Anglo-Catholicism, to form a just idea of modern England; I mean of political, social, literary England, quite as much as of religious, ecclesiastical, and moral England. If one is justified in saying that there is an England before and an England after the Reform Bill, one can and ought to say that there is an England before and an England after the *Tracts for the Times*. Tract 90, the degradation of Ward, the conversion of Newman and that of Manning, are dates not only in the history of the Oxford Movement, but also in that of England of the nineteenth century.

This explains why the English public is not weary of listening to this drama of the religious conscience. Since the day, now distant, when Newman wrote his *Apologia pro vita sua* (a masterpiece of spiritual autobiography, of psychological analysis, of intellectual subtlety, and of moral candour, worthy of figuring beside the *Confessions* of St. Augustine), how many publications of all kinds, memoirs, letters, lives, historical essays, mere articles, have been accumulated on this inexhaustible subject!

Doubtless, there still lacks the final work that will gather up these scattered threads, group these materials and raise the lasting edifice in just proportions and on firm foundations. The interesting, but incomplete and hastily-written summary by Dr. Church, Dean of St. Paul's, cannot be considered to have filled this gap. Perhaps it will never be filled. Perhaps, if it is not too presumptuous to avow such an ambition, the looked-for work will come from a most unexpected source, from outside, from a foreign hand. While waiting for this finished picture, the monumental biographies of Newman, of Pusey, and now of Manning, enable us to take in at a glance, wide sweeps of the horizon. The *Dii minores*, Keble, Ward, Richard Hurrell Froude, Robert and Henry Wilberforce, Isaac Williams, Charles Marriott, those " Twelve Good Men," whose portraits have been painted for us by Dean Burgon, have been brought into full prominence. As for Memoirs, they abound ; the Reminiscences of Palmer, the Letters of J. B. Mozley, and the gossiping and tattling Reminiscences of Oriel by Thomas Mozley, that unedifying *Ana* of a religious circle, that revelation of the private doings of a Church party, given us by a worldly ecclesiastic who was somewhat of a sceptic, in spite of, or perhaps on account of, his office.

We must put in a separate class the confessions of those who suffered shipwreck through Anglo-Catholicism; unfortunate men who fell under the influence of Newman just enough to repudiate the comfortable compromises, the easy terms of the official and established religion, and not enough to throw themselves and take a firm position upon the rock of dogmatism, the faith of authority. They caught the mystic fever only to awake shivering and depressed after the fits, and this passing attack of Catholicism allowed them to fall back into disheartened scepticism or militant agnosticism. Here is to be found Francis Newman, younger brother of John Henry, a restless, wandering spirit, at first a missionary in Persia, then a Deist in England, in all things the antitype of his glorious elder brother. He was the author of the *Phases of Faith,* and of that strange, wretched pamphlet which he felt bound to lay on the recently-closed tomb of his brother. Here also is to be seen James Anthony Froude, the historian, younger brother of Richard Hurrell. He had grown up at the feet of Newman, and was for long the most fervent and docile of disciples, but the Nemesis of Faith carried him far from that sheltered port into a stormy sea. Finally, a contrary current swept him into the arms of Carlyle, the apostle of agnostic stoicism. Healed, but feeling ever after the traces of his old wounds, he made his life-work, his *History of England in the Sixteenth Century*, a gigantic diatribe against Catholicism.

Here, too, we find Mark Pattison, at his death Rector of Lincoln College, Oxford, an embittered or rather a withered soul, less so through the disappointments and delays of his University ambitions than by his great spiritual mishap. His life's chance lost by missing the coach when he was going to abjure Protestantism with his master, he fell into systematic doubt, into the mischievous erudition of a Bayle, the haughty and superfine criticism of a Renan. As a result, the chief work of that long life of studious leisure was the volume of Memoirs where he has drawn the darkest, the most melancholy, the most painful picture of a wasted intellect, of a barren heart, voluntarily shrivelled and yet for ever inconsolable for an ideal, half-seen, half-possessed, and then for ever lost.

It is to this rich gallery that Mr. Purcell has just contributed the two ponderous volumes of his *Life of Manning*. This work has been impatiently expected. It was believed that the Cardinal had, during the last years of his life, opened the treasures of his confidence and of his papers to this writer. There was some talk of an authorized biography, and Manning's executors hardly thought they could show themselves more miserly or more timid than he; they allowed Mr. Purcell to take what he wished from the most private papers of the deceased. This book, then, constructed under such favourable circumstances, is a bad book. Manning's successor, Cardinal Vaughan, and the executors have indignantly protested against this publication. Although Mr. Purcell tries to defend himself and finds advocates among those petty minds whose chief joy is to see all greatness degraded, every impartial reader is against him. His work must be read through, if we would realize the extent to which such systematic disorder, lack of connection and of style may be carried. His book is full of fragments of letters and diaries, cut up, scattered here and there, transposed without the least attention to chronology or to association of ideas. Sometimes it is like a manuscript, whose pages, scattered by the wind, have been afterwards sewn together by an illiterate servant, sometimes a paper-basket emptied on a table. What can be said to innumerable errors that cover every page, and are truly surprising from an English, Catholic writer, devoted for years to these studies ? To imagine that Catholic Emancipation was still an unsettled question in 1830 ; persistently to call the Tractarians Puseyites before 1835, at a time when Pusey had only just openly announced his adhesion to Newman, while the honour of giving his name to this party was not his until after 1845 ; to betray at each word an inconceivable ignorance of Oxford, the affairs and the men of the University; scarcely to touch on a point of the history of Anglo-Catholicism, or even of the general religious or political history of England, without going astray in a maze of contradictions and inexactness; to disfigure many Latin quotations, and to write in a heavy style, —those are some of Mr. Purcell's faults! They would be venial in my eyes, if they were all. But it is inexcusable, that a man to whom Manning had opened the most secret treasures of his papers and his heart, who lived in familiar and constant intercourse with a great soul, should take upon himself to interlard his extracts and his abstracts with outrageous comments and insinuations; that he should systematically give an evil interpretation to all the words, acts, and even to the reticence of his hero; that he should attribute to him an equally morbid and ignoble selfishness, ambition, jealousy, duplicity, love and skill in intrigue, even cowardice; that he should draw from his own mistakes of fact or his gross confusion of ideas to calumniate him whom he claims to judge—these things, it will be confessed, surpass a reader's imagination, and I think exceed a biographer's rights. Mr. Purcell is, however, so unconscious of all this, that he professes, perhaps sincerely, great admiration for the man whom he has just treated in this way. His code of

literary propriety is also very singular. In order
to prove his gratitude to Mr. Gladstone, Manning's
former intimate ally, who made many confidences
and revelations to his friend's biographer, he bestows
upon him in passing the charming name of *Judas!*
Moreover he has not scrupled to publish documents calculated to revive the memory of old
quarrels between the dead, or provoke new ones
between the living.

Such an author puts himself out of court. History is not written in this way. As to whether
he should have been prevented from causing this
scandal, I must confess, to my shame, that I rejoice
somewhat at a few of the results of his indelicacy.
Felix culpa, since whatever may have been his intentions, Mr. Purcell (like Froude with that realistic
and impressionist *Carlyle* which so greatly shocked
the friends of the Sage of Chelsea) has given us
in a fragmentary state and complete disorder an
incomparable series of revelations and of personal
documents : a Manning painted by himself, the
involuntary avowals, the touches and retouches, the
authentic confessions of a soul of the highest order.
It is, moreover, announced that for purposes of
refutation, the executors and closest friends of the
Cardinal will shortly publish an official version of
his life. These posthumous controversies, painful
though they may be, often cast much light on the
subjects. Even after the abundant harvest, garnered

by Mr. Purcell in this indiscreet fashion, with its ill-tied sheaves, there still remain many ears to be gleaned. Meanwhile, we already possess (besides some important articles in reviews, published after Manning's death, and a small work by Miss Harriet King) the modest book by Mr. Hutton, a work from which Mr. Purcell might have learned that there is no need to have recourse to satire or to depreciation in order to avoid the continual panegyric found in the Lives of the Saints.

II

In 1832, Henry Edward Manning, then twenty-four years old, took orders and became a member of the English clergy. He had not at first felt this to be his vocation. Born on July 15, 1808, the youngest child by his second wife of a rich city merchant, Mr. William Manning, a Tory Member of Parliament, Henry Edward had been intended by his parents for the Church. The family, who belonged to the rural gentry, were respectably religious; but Manning's parents had formed this project far less through motives of piety than through the desire and hope of securing a comfortable establishment in life. The boy himself showed no taste for the profession. He was not a studious pupil either at the preparatory schools that he attended, or at Harrow, where he was sent at the age of fifteen. He was more distinguished in cricket than in his studies. Nevertheless, these four years at one of the great public schools, which with Eton, Rugby, and Winchester receive the flower of

83

English youth, were not useless to him. Wellington loved to say that the battle of Waterloo had been won on the playing-fields of Eton. In any case, that special product, the English *gentleman*, issues from these establishments, and from these alone. Manning was a gentleman, in the full force of the term, all his life long. That indescribable quality was lacking in Newman, his equal by birth, his superior in intellectual gifts, but who had not passed through one of these great schools.

In 1827, when his son left Harrow, Mr. William Manning's fortune had received some shocks. Two hundred and forty or two hundred and eighty pounds was the mininum yearly sum needed for the Oxford expenses of the young student. The father hesitated, and Manning had to promise solemnly to make up for lost time by submitting to be coached by a clergyman to whom he always afterwards attributed his sound classical knowledge and his success at Oxford. He matriculated at Balliol College, at the age of twenty. Ambitious as he was (we learn from one of his letters that he had as a motto, *Aut Cæsar aut nihil*), he determined from the outset to take rank amongst the choice spirits of his generation. His conscientious application met with its reward; in November 1830 he took a First-Class in Classics. At the same time, it was otherwise that he specially distinguished himself during those Oxford years.

The *Union* had just been started. That minia-
ture Parliament which, with its Cambridge rival,
has had as members almost every eminent man in
England, was modestly initiated, not in the sump-
tuous building where it often now invites to its
oratorical combats members of Parliament or
Ministers, but in the small rooms of the students.
Samuel Wilberforce (son of the great philanthropist),
the future English bishop, *Golden-mouthed Samuel*,
or *Soapy Sam*, according to various estimations of
him, had just resigned the presidency. William
Ewart Gladstone was about to enter on his apprenticeship to eloquence. Manning spoke much and
well; upon every subject *et de quibusdam aliis*,
from great questions of general politics to details
of home matters.

A witty, keen pen, that of the late Lord Houghton, has sketched one of the most memorable days
of this time. Cambridge has also her *Union*, and
ever at rivalry with Oxford, prided herself upon
her superiority over the *barbarians* of the other
University. On the banks of the Isis, Byron, the
poet of the age and of youth, was still cherished,
while on the shores of the Cam, the more recent
and more heterodox fame of Shelley had already
eclipsed the name of the author of *Manfred* and of
Childe Harold. On the proposal of Arthur Hallam,
the historian's son, the same whose premature death
was to secure him immortality through the elegiac

poem *In Memoriam*, a band of delegates was
charged to challenge the Byronians of Oxford in
the name of the poet of *Prometheus Unbound* and
of *Epipsychidion*. Hallam himself, Monckton
Milnes, the future Lord Houghton, essayist and
distinguished poet, lastly, Sunderland, one of those
men, great in their twentieth year, whom destiny
punishes for their precocity, went to plead their
cause. Gladstone presented the revolutionaries.
The struggle was epic, impassioned, with the highly-
spiced exaggerations, the charm and the honour
of youth. It will never be known which side
gained the victory. If the majority of votes fell to
Manning, uncompromising defender of Byron, he
declared later that the arguments of the three
Shelleyites had routed him.

Those happy days of study for its own sake,
generous enthusiasm, pure friendship, pass only too
quickly. Practical life must be entered upon.
Manning's vocation was very decided at that time.
Politics attracted him, and fully occupied his
thoughts. He dreamed of Parliament, oratorical
success, power, action. He already saw himself
Prime Minister, and if his fellow-students had
drawn his horoscope and that of Gladstone, they
would have reserved for the latter the mitre and
crozier, and given to the future Archbishop of
Westminster the seals of State. Fate decided
otherwise. Mr. W. Manning was ruined. Broken-

hearted, he was obliged to go through the Bank-
ruptcy Court, send in his resignation as Director of
the Bank of England, of which he had been for
some time Governor, accept the Chiltern Hundreds,
and sell his fine country-house. It was not possible
with the crumbs of the father's fortune to bear the
cost of a parliamentary career, such as was dreamt
of by Manning; for in England a man places his
leisure and his income at the service of his country,
instead of earning his living or making his fortune
in office. Manning, down-hearted, had to accept
from the careless patronage of Lord Goderich a
very humble post as supernumerary in the Colonial
Office.

He was urged to reflect, to choose the Church
rather than enter a Government office through
this side-door. He refused. His religious feelings
were not vivid; he had none of those strange
presentiments, that natural, almost morbid, mysti-
cism, that hidden, ardent, spiritual life, like St.
Theresa, that kind of half-waking dream, of which
Newman has left us a never-to-be-forgotten picture,
and which singled him out, as by a miracle, while
still in the midst of Protestantism, for Catholicism
and the priesthood. The awakening of the religious
conscience, *conversion*, to use the technical term of
Protestant psychology, was in Manning's case the
effect of feminine influence. He was intimate with
a great City banker's family, the Bevans. Miss

Bevan had a very religious mind, deeply impregnated with the piety and theology of the Evangelical School, whose influence I shall have to describe. She read the Bible, she prayed with the young man, in short, she was God's instrument in touching that heart and conquering that soul. This was only a beginning. Manning dated his true and complete conversion from his illness of 1847, but the seed had been sown none the less.

It is interesting to notice, in passing, that the two leaders of the English Catholic Restoration owed their spiritual birth to Evangelicalism, and made no secret of it. For years Newman was a zealous adherent, not only of the religious school, but also of the ecclesiastical party of that name. He founded and directed at Oxford for some time one of those special institutions of that form of Protestantism, an auxiliary committee of the Bible Society. In his *Apologia*, where he weighed each phrase, he declared that he owed, in some measure, *his soul*, the word is strong, to Scott's ultra-Protestant Commentary on the Bible. Manning also kept up a connection, even after he had openly joined the Oxford Movement, with some of the chief members of the Evangelical party. This is an important fact. These two Cardinals, these two athletes of Catholicism, have not only begun as Protestants, but as the most Protestant of Protestants. Their testimony shows that both retained a remembrance, even more, an indelible trace of this fact. Certainly, when they submitted to the Church, by that very act they repudiated everything that in their eyes made for the errors and the sin of schism and heresy; still, the experience of the past remained with them of necessity. They knew for themselves all the excellence and truth that can be found in a false system; they knew that even in militant, uncompromising Protestantism, provided only it keep faith in the Gospel, and docility to revelation, there exists the germ of all truths, even those which it rejects and which form the crown of Catholicism. Certain polemical methods to which controversy too often stoops on the Continent, would have been quite impossible for them.

At this date, however, Manning had not yet got to this point. He had just received the spark which was to kindle in him the sacred fire of the Spirit, never more to be extinguished. His father's ruin, with all that it brought after it for him, was the first call to a higher vocation. A private grief, the refusal of a prudent father to sanction the marriage, more dreamed of than proposed, of a young supernumerary at the Colonial Office with his daughter, completed the work already begun. Heavenly voices made themselves audible. He thus described his state of mind, in a letter of this time, to his confidant, his brother-in-law—"sick, savage, sour, rabid, indolent, ill at ease"; that he felt a need "to be anywhere but where I am, to do or hear anything but what I do or hear; in fine, be anything, body, monster, beast, or creature, but what I am." "All things are false, whether made of body, or soul, or mechanism and clap-trap. Why, look ye now! there's philosophy; vitæ magistra, doctrinarum excultrix, artium indagatrix, etc. When all is snug and warm and comfortable, she's the trustiest friend, companion, counsellor, comforter, and protector, but when matters take an angry aspect—whiff! she's off with her tail in the air, like a robustious cow in sultry weather."

It was only a well-known form of a malady of youth; a fit of Byronism or sharp Wertherism, complicated by a very natural state of depression at the sight of that world, all of whose openings were closed to the hopes or the ambitions of his twenty-five years.

Later, Manning could distinguish the providential hand that brought upon him all these disappointments at the very time when an inner work had begun in his soul, the voice that spoke to him so clearly and so loudly. He resolved, he tells us so himself, "not to be a clergyman in the sense of my old destiny, but to give up the world and to live for God and for souls. I had been praying much, and going much to churches. It was a turning-point in my life."

I pity those who, like Mr. Purcell and certain of his critics, see only a kind of last resource and worldly speculation in the decision which Manning himself recorded in these simple, beautiful words— "It was a call from God, as all that He has given me since. It was a call *ad veritatem et ad se ipsum.*"

The proof that he did not obey purely human views is, as he has remarked, that "the thought of being a clergyman was positively repulsive to me. I had an intense recoil from the secularity of the Established Church. The sight of an apron and shovel hat literally provoked me. The title 'Father in God' applied to bishops living in ease irritated me. My one thought was to obey God's will, to save my soul and the souls of others."

Manning was fortunate enough to be placed from the beginning in an extremely comfortable position. Scarcely had he been ordained by the Bishop of Oxford, after the short preparation that in those days was sufficient for the English clergy, than he became, in January 1833, one of the curates of the Reverend John Sargent, Rector of Lavington, his relation by marriage. The eldest of the daughters of the house had already married Samuel Wilberforce, recently made rector of a parish in the Isle of Wight. It was these young ladies' destiny to reward the zeal of their father's curates. After a few months, the youngest, Caroline, became

Manning's wife. In the month of May, Manning, at the death of his father-in-law, was presented to the important living by his betrothed's grand-mother, who was mistress of the manor-house, and had the living in her gift. At the age of twenty-five, after only a few weeks' apprenticeship, Manning found himself in the position of beneficed clergy-man, to which so many of his fellows never reach. Married, with a settled income, highly placed, he was in the most enviable of positions.

This very happiness had its dangers. Who knows, in case it had been prolonged, whether the Rector of Lavington, the husband of an accom-plished wife, perhaps surrounded by children, possessing a comfortable income, at the head of an important parish, on the road to high offices, might not have descended to the level of those comfort-able, respectable, honourable, benevolent, well-paid, well-fed clergy, who are often good fathers of families, seldom ascetics or saints, and believe more in the wise precepts of orthodox political economy than in the divine madness of charity? God kept him from that peril. He left him the externals of that happiness, that high position, that luxury, those horses he loved, and in whose knowledge he was a past-master; He left him all that outside shell (that Manning himself firmly put aside as soon as he had taken his first step in the path of renunciation), but He struck him to the heart.

After four years of cloudless happiness, his wife was taken from him. Manning never allowed any one to sound the depths of his grief. Some feelings are too sacred to be spoken of; Manning was never one of those who profane the privacy of their memories, who turn the sanctuary of their affections into a public place. Never, even while serving a Church that permits her clergy to marry, even in his correspondence with his nearest relations, even in his private diary, did he make a direct allusion to his loss. He briefly mentions this date—July 21, 1837, only in the list of merciful dispensations by which God led him to Himself. Later, other reasons made his silence more unbroken; as a Catholic priest, the head of a celibate clergy, it would not have been fitting for him to awaken this memory.

If we may believe a legend, perhaps unauthentic, others took this task upon themselves. During vehement and sometimes envenomed struggles, which he had to maintain against certain factions in the midst of Catholicism, an old priest, detesting the new *régime*, was accustomed to keep as a day of mourning the anniversary of Mrs. Manning's death, and when he was asked the reason, he replied—"It is the date of the hardest blow that God has struck the Church in the British Isles in our day."[1]

[1] Mr. Purcell, in a note on p. 310, vol. ii., mentions that,

Even while married Manning never spent his days in idle comfort. Besides indefatigable parochial activity, he did not delay to enter on the great struggle that was occupying all minds.

---

some one having said, "Newman's conversion was the greatest calamity that the Catholic Church has experienced in our time," Canon MacMullen replied—"No, the greatest misfortune for the Church of our time was the death of a woman (Mrs. Manning)." I have personal reasons for not believing this anecdote too implicitly, nor a subsequent dialogue between the Cardinal and the Canon, that seems to be apocryphal.

IT was the solemn time when the Oxford Movement broke out with the sound of war. The Established Church of England, through the strange anomalies of her origin, had always in herself the germs of two contradictory systems, Catholicism and Protestantism. The struggle between these two opposing elements disturbed the whole of the first half of the seventeenth century. Archbishop Laud was an Anglo-Catholic too early. He formed a fatal alliance with that unlucky dynasty of the Stuarts, and expiated on the scaffold his complicity with Strafford and Charles I., in their abortive attempt at absolute government without a Parliament, rather than his hostility against triumphant Puritanism. Anglican theology with Hooker, with Bull, with those non-jurors who made the mistake of setting up as a dogma the purely human and political doctrine of Divine Right and non-resistance, still continuing to repudiate Protestantism and its inspirations. In the eighteenth century, with

95

the definite victory of the Revolution of 1688, and the establishment of the House of Hanover, came the accession of all the powers of spiritual death, of Erastianism, or the absolute subordination of the Church to the State, of practical materialism, formalism, rationalism, that faint-hearted Christianity that is afraid of its own shadow, that dreads and forbids nothing so much as enthusiasm, that is reduced to a system of purely civil morality, and keeps a cowardly silence on revealed dogma. It was truly the sleep of death.

At last came a revival of faith, zeal, ardour, generous imprudence. It was outside the English Church. John Wesley indeed remained to the end her faithful and devoted son. If he founded a new sect—Methodism—whose followers are now reckoned by millions in the Anglo-Saxon world, it was in spite of himself. He wished to awaken consciences, save souls, preach the eternal Gospel, but, thanks to the intolerance of the English Church, he found that he had created another. In the beginnings of Methodism, there was something of the grandeur and simplicity of Early Christianity, or if that is too strong a comparison, of the foundation of the Mendicant Orders. Its apostles had the power of setting simple emotions in vibration in the hearts of the people, the common chords of the consciousness of sin and longing for repentance. The effect of this powerful movement was felt even in the English Church. Methodism, Wesley, were the authors of that beneficent reaction of Evangelicalism that brought some religious vitality into the Church of England. There has been no more characteristic product of Protestantism than Evangelicalism; the same greatness and pettiness, the same qualities and defects, are apparent in both. Strictly individualistic, it appealed especially to religious emotions. Its great object was conversion, viewed, not as the slow and progressive action of the Spirit of God, working through every means of ordinary and extraordinary grace upon a human being, but as an indivisible point in time and space, the sudden transformation of a soul, the miraculous and instantaneous deliverance which breaks asunder the yoke of sin. From the beginning, in spite of the great things done or called forth by the new school, to which eloquent homage was formerly rendered by M. de Remusat, it showed serious and fatal blanks. It lacked the sense of penitence in the tragic meaning of that word for an Augustine, a Saint-Cyran, or a Pascal. It lacked the conception of the Church, of the Sacraments, the consciousness of human unity and of Divine authority. Finally, it lacked a theology, the understanding of dogma, and of its fitting place in a supernatural and revealed religion.

Still, these defects showed themselves only after a time. At the beginning, Evangelicalism proved

H

itself to be a power of life and progress. A Divine breath brought together and revivified the scattered bones of Anglican formalism. The clergy ceased to be, according to the clever and too exact expression of J. de Maistre, a company of gentlemen dressed in black, who, on Sunday, utter moral things from the pulpit. The clergyman described, not without some exaggeration, by Macaulay, the humble parasite of manor-houses, the destined husband of my Lady's waiting-woman, or worse still, of my Lord's cast-off mistress, Fielding's parson, famishing spunger, literary Bohemian, or poor country vicar with a miserable allowance, even the rectors and vicars so admirably depicted in their novels by Jane Austen or later by George Eliot, those robust, jolly, country gentlemen, ever the first at the meet, knowing more of the mysteries of sport or the turf than of theology, all these old-world clergy, antediluvian fauna, began to disappear under the influence of Evangelicalism.

The reaction did not stop there. The laity were still more closely touched by it. There was a magnificent outburst of great charitable enterprises. It will be to the eternal honour of this teaching, which seemed, by its narrow conception of Salvation through Faith, certain to paralyze all religious activity, that it raised a crop of Christian works, *i. e.* missions to the heathen, thus removing from Protestantism the reproach of neglecting one of Christ's commands; societies for charitable purposes, for education of the people, prison reform, above all, that excellent movement against the slave trade and slavery with which the name of Wilberforce is identified.

Such is the record that Evangelicalism can show. It left indelible traces, not only in the history, but also in the moral and intellectual constitution of the English people. Towards the end of the first quarter of this century it was at the zenith of its power and success. Its heroic age was now ended. This great current of enthusiasm was about to slacken, to become sluggish and stagnant.

In its turn, victorious Evangelicalism, cherished and professed by those who formerly persecuted it, ran the risk of becoming Pharisaical. It fell back into formalism, but into a formalism a hundred times worse, because the affectation of certain sentiments was hypocrisy, and because it lacked, in compensation, the ample traditions, the wide prospects, the intrinsic strength of the sacraments of the Anglo-Catholic system.

It was just the time when the progress of Liberalism seemed to place in peril again ecclesiastical establishments, if not the Church. After the philosophy of the eighteenth century, and its commonplace rationalism, thought and knowledge had progressed, and men now saw the first attempts at that Higher Criticism, that German criticism with which Pusey came into contact during that University pilgrimage whence he was to bring such a curious book. In politics, the hour was approaching when the Whigs triumphed, after half-a-century of Tory government and determined resistance to all spiritual or temporal novelty. The spirit of toleration, wrongly confounded with the spirit of sceptical indifference, had, thanks to the *great treason* of Peel and Wellington, just gained a decisive victory in the question of Catholic Emancipation, and was about to abolish the tests or religious oaths. The Liberals openly avowed their intention of reforming the Church, suppressing bishoprics and prebends, of revising revenues and endowments, and abolishing tithes. The voice of one in a very high position had just summoned the bishops to set their house in order. Lastly, the invasion of society by that middle-class, infected by the leprosy of Nonconformity, the growing shadow thrown by Continental revolutions on the island-kingdom, all these things terrified the devout. The younger clergy, in particular, felt called to a holy war.

These champions cast their eyes around them to discover means of defence. In the official arsenal of the Establishment they found only the rusty, blunted, worn-out weapons of State religion and political orthodoxy. As for Evangelicalism, it compromised on one side with the enemy by

taking the Holy Communion with schismatics of
Protestant Dissent ; on the other, it presented only
badly-tempered weapons, which were shivered at
first contact with the double-edged, sharp blades
of Catholic controversy or revolutionary polemics.
If the Church of England were to be saved, her
title-deeds must be found and restored to her.   If
she were to be protected from human action,
the supernatural powers of her Divine mission
must be hers once more.   If she were anything
else than the creature of the State, at the mercy of
the holders of temporal power, her spiritual power
must be restored, she must be led back to her
supernatural sources, and those marks of authenticity
that make a Church, and without which there is no
Church, must once more be brought to light.

Some young men, mostly Fellows of Oriel
College, Oxford, were eager to enter the field.
Keble, formerly distinguished by a University
career of unparalleled brilliancy, had retired to a
country parish, where a ray of fame had visited
him after the publication of his poems, the *Christian Year*. On July 14, 1833, he preached the
Assize Sermon at Oxford, that sermon upon
national apostasy that Newman always considered
the first blast of the trumpet of the holy war.
Newman had lately returned from that journey to
Italy and Sicily which was brightened by mysterious presentiments and saddened by superstitious

fears, nearly bringing him to the grave. He had come into contact with the religion of the Catholic world, and he had felt something of the simple terror and the scruples of a child reared in another sanctuary. He returned with the intuition, still vague, of a great mission, the zeal of a renewed consecration.

Amongst the friends to whom he revealed these secret thoughts, it was R. Hurrell Froude who had the most decisive influence over him. Already attacked by that consumption to which he fell a prey, Froude had the feverish haste of a man whose days are numbered. Brought up in the purest High Church traditions by his father, the Archdeacon, he had gathered together some fragments of the Anglo-Catholic inheritance from those two forerunners, Alexander Knox and Bishop Jebb. He was much nearer the Catholic Church than was the Protestant Newman, descended by his mother from Huguenot refugees, and reared in an Evangelical atmosphere. At this time Newman still looked upon Rome as the great "whore of the Apocalypse," and upon the Pope as Antichrist. His imagination, saturated with the metaphors of Protestant controversy, persistently suggested to him these grotesque analogies, even when his reason and conscience drew him near to Catholicism.

At the outset of his work, when he began the

publication of *Tracts for the Times*, he was quite free from even a secret predilection for Rome. He rather opposed in her the great enemy who compromised truth when she did not corrupt it, and whose undertakings, superfetations, and systematic usurpations explained, if they did not justify, the errors, mutilations, and negations of Protestantism.

Relying upon his theory, which he believed to be invincible, of conformity to the primitive Church, and of the unchanging trust of the Faith, Newman unhesitatingly threw down a challenge to these two formidable powers, Catholicism and Protestantism. Not only did he think it possible to trace between the two forms of error a *via media* equally distant from each, but in his eyes the Established Church monopolized the truth and the whole truth. Strange and noble illusion of a purely intellectual genius! Newman started in search of the best means of defence of the Church that was dear to him, and he had concluded that the surest as well as the simplest means was to claim for her the supernatural marks of *the* Church. A purely national, insular Church, separated from the rest of the world, submissive to the civil authority, pervaded with the doctrines and the rites of the Reformation—he claimed for her all the signs of the one eternal, immutable, infallible, visible Church—that is to say, according to the formula of Vincent de Lérins, "semper, ubique, ab omnibus"; such was the desperate enterprise to which a young unknown Fellow of Oriel vowed himself one day in the year of grace 1833. On this foundation he raised the pile of the *Tracts for the Times*, those little periodical pamphlets which he inspired, revised, for whose publication he was responsible, and of which he was most often the author.

The success of these loose sheets was prodigious. A great party, of whom Newman was the leader, was immediately formed, and he became famous and powerful. He entered upon that extraordinary period of his life that lasted for twelve years, and whose halting-places he has himself noted down as the Stations of the Cross. England had the unprecedented spectacle of a plain clergyman, who held no position in the hierarchy, becoming the commander-in-chief of a great army, the absolute master of devoted friends, the infallible oracle of a school, the director of the consciences of a crowd of penitents. It has been said that at that time the adequate and complete formula of the faith of many men, eminent in judgment and will, was these words—*Credo in Newmanum*. His sermons at St. Mary's, the University Church, were attended by immense audiences. His modest rooms at Oriel were a sanctuary whose threshold could not be crossed without emotion. A word from him, even less than that, a passing shade of expression, a gesture, a silent pause, were obeyed or listened to, as the commands of a king or the decrees of an infallible pontiff. Rarely has a man in this or any other age enjoyed more fully the intoxicating joys of an intellectual and moral dictatorship.

What is pathetic in his case is, that during almost all this time the object of this adoration, the idol of this worship, was a prey to the poignant anguish of doubt. He saw sinking under his feet the very soil on which he was erecting this imposing edifice. He saw an abyss open beside him, and, more unfortunate than Pascal, it was he who brought to it all those who confided in him. His dialectics held him in a pitiless vice. Starting from the premisses he had laid down, and which were applauded by the unconscious crowd, he was led on to conclusions before which his whole soul recoiled terrified, conclusions which he hated, which overthrew his work, but from which he could not honestly withdraw.

Newman has left us in his *Apologia* and in a still more direct and living form, his *Letters*, the story of this spiritual experience. Very soon he felt that he had not the right to limit his affirmations to what was useful to his cause. It would have been very convenient, but not sufficiently honest, to cut off from his theories all that went beyond the current conception of Anglicanism, to prune away all that threatened the claims or showed the contradictions of the Church of England. Accepting, invoking a part of the formula of Vincent de Lérins, he could not conscientiously reject and condemn the remainder. Did not his doctrine of the rule of Christian antiquity, of conformity to the primitive Church, logically imply Catholicism? How could he assert with the same breath that the Church was by divine right the depository and interpreter of revealed truth, and that she was the mistress of errors and sponsor of popular superstitions? With what right could he proclaim the infallible authority of the Church of the first three centuries, of the great Œcumenical Councils, only to recognize the great defection of the Church in the Middle Ages, the straying from the right path of the Council of Trent.

The terror with which Newman saw the uprising of these questions was sincere. If his mind began to throw off the yoke of his Protestant prejudices, his heart and imagination were still enslaved by them. Before him arose this dilemma : in the midst of songs of triumph and cries of joy, to continue on the foundations he had laid, to construct the majestic Anglican cathedral ; but then, to go on to the end, to crown its top with the cross of St. Peter and to submit to Rome ; or firmly to reject the Papal claims, unwaveringly to repudiate the extreme consequences of the Catholic system—but then, in that case, to avow openly that the intermediate theory of the *via media* was wrong, that the whole Tractarian enterprise had started from a false point of departure, and that Geneva was right. It is easy to imagine the tragic element in this state of a party-leader, consumed by these thoughts at the very moment and partly on account of his successes.

It seemed to Newman, thus driven back upon himself, that he was doomed to strike a deadly blow at his mother, the Church ; whether he forsook her to kneel before her proud enemy, or whether he tore away from her with his own hands the crown that he had just placed upon her head. This inner strife was already far advanced when, as a climax, there came a whole series of external facts, of undeniable, practical realities, which showed him the fictitious and imaginary elements of his fundamental affirmations. It was no longer a question of knowing theoretically whether a Church possessing, or claiming a part of the supernatural attributes of the ideal Church, has the logical right to repudiate the others. Newman had either to shut his eyes to facts or to deduce from them the inevitable consequences.

In spite of the almost miraculous propagation of his doctrine, or rather on account of that same diffusion that provoked conflicts and brought forth opposition, Newman had to own that Anglicanism did not possess the distinctive signs of the Church of God. How could such fictions as the following be maintained, when every fact gave the lie to them?—fictions, such as an inspired witness to revelation, an inviolable depository of dogma, a faithful administrator of the sacraments, an Episcopate in direct line of Apostolic succession—how could they be maintained when the Church of England suffered and accepted the appointment of a heretic, Hampden, as Regius Professor of Theology; when she bestirred herself only to condemn baptismal regeneration, too strictly taught by Pusey, or the too Catholic system of interpretation of Tract 90, or the impetuous Ward and his Ideal Church; when the Episcopacy gave over to the civil power the keys of the citadel, finding energy only to fire upon its own troops and show severity against the too zealous faithful?

From that time, Newman himself tells us he was on his death-bed. For five years longer the death-struggle went on; he stoutly resisted the call which urged him to throw himself at the feet of the Vicar of Christ. His old instincts, his bringing-up, the sorrow of being the destroyer of his life's work; the grief of seeming to justify by a crowning act the odious calumnies that accused him of Jesuitically masking his true design and of deliberately doing the work of Catholicism; the ties of family and friendship, the fear of scandalizing faithful hearts and docile spirits; the remembrance of the graces received when in communion with the Anglican Church, that filial piety that does not die out in a day, even when a man has learnt that the mother who carried him in her arms is not his true mother, —all these feelings taken together surged in him, tortured and kept him back.

In order to justify in his own eyes this obstinate resistance, he took refuge in the most desperate resolutions, the subtlest and even the most sophistical expedients. At one time he found some relief in the mystical theory of the Babylonish captivity. In his eyes the Established Church was sick, a slave to civil power, a prey to error; it was her children's duty all the same to live and die in her bosom, that is to say, deprived of the graces granted to more favoured communions, but with the bitter satisfaction of being obedient to the end, and faithful in spite of all. This ingenious expedient ceased to satisfy him the day when he perceived that by this subterfuge he merely came back to Protestant individualism and to the suppression of the Church as a means of grace. In the main, his decision was taken when he clearly saw that he was held back, less by the scruples of his conscience, the doubts of his reason, or the affections of his heart, than by the apprehension of a party leader, the annoyances of the humiliated teacher, the point of honour of the general obliged to go over to the enemy.

He had untied, one after the other, the threads connecting him with the past. He ceased to reside at Oriel College; he resigned his cure of the University Church of St. Mary; he had put an end, by order of his bishop, to the series of *Tracts for the Times;* he gave up the editorship of his review, *The British Critic.* Finally, he retired to Littlemore, a hamlet near Oxford, into a kind of hermitage, or small monastery, that he had built, and where, surrounded by a band of young disciples, he led, for two or three years, a cloistered and monastic life.

Events hurried on. Bunsen, the Prussian Minister, unconsciously gave the last impulse to a slowly-formed resolution, by obtaining the assent of the English Church and Government to his favourite plan of creating a half-Anglican, half-Prussian bishopric at Jerusalem. This was a patent, avowed act of co-operation, almost of fusion, with Continental Protestantism. The long death-struggle came to an end in the autumn of 1845. On October 8, Newman abjured Protestantism, was received into the Catholic Church, and communicated from the hands of Father Dominic, an Italian, a Passionist Father, who was passing through England, formerly a shepherd from the Roman Campagna.

IV

I HAVE thus sketched the Oxford Movement up to the final catastrophe. The mere fact that I could follow its course without once mentioning Manning's name sufficiently proves that, although he felt its influence profoundly, he did not at this time play an important part in it. Newman in himself constituted Tractarianism, but neither Manning's temperament nor the circumstances of his existence at that time disposed him to take a chief part at the outset of the Anglo-Catholic agitation. He was always far less a man of books, a theorist, a theologian, than a man of action and authority. The archdeaconry of Chichester, in which he exercised for eighteen years his parochial functions under four bishops, was widely different from the atmosphere of Oxford.

Yet Manning had not neglected, through the medium of common friends, to place himself in connection with Newman. The principles of the new school appealed to one side of his nature, and separating himself from the Evangelical party, he enlisted in the Anglican ranks. The first sermon he published was the official proclamation of this fact, and in it he discussed the *Rule of Faith*. His fundamental affirmations, his developments of the subjects, especially the notes with which he amplified it, bore the stamp of the new doctrine, and revealed the fact that he had submitted the proofs of his work to Newman. The Evangelical party were greatly excited. Their organ, *The Record*, passed a severe reprimand on this "new wolf in sheep's clothing." The Bishop of Chester pronounced a diatribe against him. Manning had joined the Tractarian ranks.

All his friendships inclined him to this direction. After Robert Wilberforce, perhaps his most intimate friend, and sharer of all his opinions, and Henry Wilberforce, his brother-in-law, he was most closely connected with Mr. Gladstone, then a young member of the House of Commons, "the hope of uncompromising young Toryism," as he was called by Macaulay. In a journey to Rome, in 1838, the first of the many visits that Manning paid to the Eternal City, he had the young statesman as a companion. They visited Dr. Wiseman together, who was far from suspecting that his successor to the Archiepiscopal throne of Westminster stood before him in the person of the young English clergyman. Together they visited the churches, and heard a father of the order of preaching friars, whose sermon, popular yet dogmatic, made Mr. Gladstone feel jealous for Anglicanism. They walked together one fine Sunday on the Piazza de Fiore, when the Rector of Lavington, stricter on this point than in his later Roman days, severely reproved Mr. Gladstone for the grave fault of having bought apples on the Sabbath.

In 1840, at the age of thirty-two, Manning received promotion to the important post of Archdeacon of Chichester. It was the moment when Newman in the Tractarian camp betrayed, in spite of himself, his inner struggle, and when a band of audacious young men, with Ward at their head, noisily proclaimed their contempt for the Reformation and their love for Catholicism. Manning had always been more of a Protestant than his Oxford ally. It had never cost him anything, even while professing the principles of the new school, to render homage or justice to those Reformers of the sixteenth century whose names seemed to scald the lips of some Tractarians, and whom Ward unhesitatingly sent to everlasting flames.

In fact, there was never full harmony or perfect sympathy between Newman and Manning, even during this honeymoon of their connection, nor

later, though Manning, having become a Catholic,
found it his duty to dedicate a book to Newman,
"as to the master to whom he owed more gratitude
than to any other man." As long as both were
Protestants, Newman was by far the more Catholic
of the two. There is a simple but coarse way of
explaining this mystery. Mr. Purcell feels no
doubt that Manning, a servant of circumstances,
a worshipper of the rising sun, an enemy of
lost causes (I quote my author), always took
the side he thought the strongest, always ran
with the hare and hunted with the hounds.
This solution of the problem presents, among
other defects, that of leaving Newman's conduct
totally unexplained, in traversing the same road
as Manning, but in the opposite direction. The
true key seems to be the contrast of these two
natures.

One is the very type of the intellectual man,
struggling with his own conceptions, I might almost
say with the phantoms of his mind, inclined through
scrupulousness and subtlety to throw doubt upon
what attracts him, to mistrust his own postulates,
to saw off the branch on which he is standing. The
other is, in all the force of the term, a man of action,
for whom ideas are not the counters of an infinitely
subtle and complicated game, but the bases of
operations, the foundations on which to build.
Just as the first will be doomed to examine his

credo under every aspect, to search anxiously for its weak points, especially to see the inequalities and cracks in the ground on which he has taken his position, so will the second, through need of certainty, through practical necessity, be faithful to his premisses, and proceed straight to their logical conclusions. His Protestantism will be, so long as it lasts, as robust as his later Catholicism, and both will be equally sincere.

It was thus through conviction, and not though policy, that Manning at this time was far more Antiroman than most of his party. He wrote to Pusey to thank him for some words he had written, but "especially for the passages the most opposed to Rome." He added that "his conscience was tortured at the thought of that turning aside of affection, that sacrilegious transfer of the hearts of men from the only object of worship to the Virgin Mary." In his eyes, a letter of Dr. Wiseman's, that had lately appeared, "sufficed to condemn the whole Catholic system;" the parallel "between the feelings of a child for his mother and those of the faithful for the Virgin" seemed "frightful" to him. His tone of language with regard to Catholicism differed radically, not only from, so to speak, the light cavalry of the party, but from the grave doctors, from those who, like Pusey, were to remain Anglicans to the end.

On November 5, 1844, to repudiate all responsibility for what he considered the loose casuistry of Tract 90, he accepted the offer of preaching a sermon before the University, in honour of the double Protestant Anniversary of the Gunpowder Plot, and the landing of William of Orange in 1688. This proceeding, called by some a cowardly defection, was only the faithful application of his principles. If Manning could not conscientiously have called himself a Protestant, he would not have remained a single day in a Communion that was Protestant by law and in fact. Some of his friends blamed him for this manifestation. Newman, whom he visited at Littlemore the next day, would have shut the door in his face, if we may believe a story, very doubtful, however, as the correspondence between the two was never interrupted, and the Rector of Lavington was amongst those few to whom Father Dominic's neophyte communicated his final resolution.

Moreover, he was so positively looked upon as one of the champions of Anglo-Catholicism, that his opponents drew no distinction between him and those who held extreme Catholic views. When Blomfield, the Bishop of London, was told of Manning's journey to Rome, he exclaimed, " To Rome ! I thought since the publication of his sermon that he was there already." These suspicions, and the cavils of the Evangelical party,

scarcely fettered the activity of the Archdeacon of
Chichester. His charges treated fully and authoritatively of the great questions of the day. The
Essay on the Unity of the Church (published in
1842, with a dedication to Mr. Gladstone) rapidly
became one of the classics of Anglicanism. Phill-
potts, the famous Bishop of Exeter, said—"We
have three men on whom we can rely—Gladstone
in the State; Hope (Sir Walter Scott's grandson
by marriage) at the Bar; Manning in the Church;"
he added, "No power on earth can prevent Manning
from becoming a bishop." A religious newspaper,
the *Christian Remembrancer*, shared this opinion,
and declared that the young archdeacon was "one
of those men of whom the Church has need for
her highest offices, and who cannot grow old in the
honourable posts they occupy."

At Littlemore, on the eve of Newman's submission, the opinion was equally shared (according
to the testimony of Father Lockhart), that Manning was destined for the Episcopate. Frederick
Denison Maurice (an opponent, and the eminent
leader of the Liberal party of the English Broad
Church), after a short stay under the same
roof, exclaimed—"I do not know where, in our
day, could be found a better or wiser bishop."
Some years later, after an important meeting, he
wrote—"There was in that room a man who
could save the Church, if he would; that one is

Manning." In his diary, Manning owned to himself "that his foot was upon the lowest rung of the ladder that he had so greatly desired."

Therefore, when at last the crisis came, when "that inexplicable event," according to Lord John Russell, occurred, when Newman by his conversion inflicted, as Disraeli said, "a shock upon England, under which she still reels," when daily, weekly, men learnt the defection of Ward, Dalgairns, Oakeley, of almost all the *aides-de-camp* of the Littlemore recluse, the eyes of all, friends and enemies, instinctively turned towards Manning as towards Pusey. They seemed to be the destined leaders of a new campaign; a campaign where they must pass from the offensive to the defensive, where there was no longer need of brilliant and adventurous soldiers in the vanguard, but of men of authority and rulers. Manning was keenly affected. He had written to Newman a farewell letter, assuring him that "if he knew words that could express his deep love for him, *without sullying his conscience,* he would gladly use them," and while deploring the impossibility of their ever again meeting at the same altar in this life, hoped for a re-union in the next world.

He foresaw the gravity of the crisis. The day when he had been present at the degradation of Ward by the University of Oxford, he turned towards Gladstone and said in a low voice, "'Αρχὴ

ὠδίνων; this is the beginning of sorrows." He
knew not then what a true prophet he was. While
Gladstone (who had enough confidence in him to
write : " I begin to think that, on a matter of importance, I cannot differ from you ") wished " the
trumpet to give no uncertain sound," Manning
became a prey to cruel uncertainty. For him as
for Newman, a mysterious, providential destiny
ordained that the hour of doubt should coincide
with the hour of triumph. Could he have kept to
the end the serene and absolute faith that made
him condemn Newman's conversion as a sin, and
astonish Gladstone by attributing to "a want of
truth," these submissions to Rome, he would have
been happier and stronger. Two days after Newman's *great treason*, he could still assert to an intimate friend that " nothing in the world could shake
his faith in the presence of Christ in our Church
and sacraments."

This certainty is indispensable to a man of action
at the very time when he is called to defend the
most sacred of causes. The anguish of losing it
little by little was not spared him. On the one
hand, he saw himself compelled to own the
insoluble contradictions between the theory of
Anglo-Catholicism and the realities of the Established Church. On the other hand, the continual
progress of his inner and spiritual life, his increased
mystical piety, his pastoral zeal, his asceticism, his

holiness, created in him fresh needs to which the English Church could offer only illusory satisfaction, but which the Catholic Church was fully able to gratify. In 1846 he noted in his diary that the English Church, in his opinion, was organically and functionally unhealthy; that with regard to her organization, she was separated from the Universal Church and the See of Peter, subjected without power of appeal to the civil power, stripped of the sacrament of penance and of the daily sacrifice of the Eucharist, deprived of the Minor Orders, and furnished with a mutilated ritual; that, from the second point of view, she had no longer either daily service or discipline, neither unity in devotion nor in ritual, neither preparatory education for her clergy nor sacerdotal life among her bishops and priests, neither hold over the consciences of the people nor faith in the mysteries of the invisible world.

Manning ceaselessly reiterated this formidable indictment during five long years. He reproached his own Church with lacking "antiquity, system, intelligibility, order, strength, unity." He deplored "these dogmas on paper only," this ritual universally forsaken, this clergy and laity widely divided. He sadly repeated, "Although I am not a Roman Catholic, I have ceased to be an Anglican." He struggled against himself, unceasingly resuming the examination of his conscience, questioning himself whether he was not a prey to the tempter's snares, whether he ought not to mistrust himself and look upon those who until then had remained in the Anglican faith as more humble than those who had left it. At the same time, he was obliged to say that "nothing in Rome repelled him enough to keep him apart, whilst nothing in Protestantism attracted him enough to retain him."

In July 1846 he wrote—"The chief thing is the attraction of Rome, which satisfies me fully—reason, feeling, my whole nature—whilst the English Church affords only an approximate satisfaction, and even that only through the supplementary means which we bring to her."

He wrote these curious words, that are at the same time an implied protest and the confession of an irresistible fascination—"The net closes its meshes around me." A little later we find—"I feel as if a great light had shone before my eyes. My feeling with regard to Roman Catholicism does not arise from the intellect. I have intellectual difficulties, but the great moral difficulties are on the point of melting. Something stirs in me and repeats—'You will die a Catholic.'" Uneasy about his future, he asked himself—"How can I know where I shall be at the end of two years? Where was Newman five years ago? May it not be that I shall have reached the same point as he?" According to his expression, "strange thoughts visited him." In his opinion, the theory of the Oxford School manifestly contradicted the West and the East. Anglicanism implied, on the one side, principles which justified Protestantism, and which Lutherans and Calvinists had the right to invoke against it ; on the other side, it implied principles that necessarily led to Catholicism. The whole Ango-Catholic movement rested equally on a contradiction ; it was a question of Catholicizing the Church, that is, that some of the faithful should be a means of grace for the sole means of supreme grace, that the children should bring forth the mother, that the individualistic method of Protestantism should be employed to restore Catholicism. Finally, in spite of these attempts at renovation, the English Establishment, muti- lated, devastated, ruined at the Reformation, remained incapable of offering an asylum to penitents and a refuge to Christ's disciples.

His diary, his letters to Robert Wilberforce and to Mr. Gladstone, are full of these sad avowals. Nevertheless, Manning, like Newman, whose intel- lectual temperament he did not possess, would have prolonged his resistance to these doubts even still further, if he had had to fight against them only. He felt an invincible terror and repugnance at the thought of leaving his Church. "Of all things in the world," he wrote, "it is the most like death to me." What a picture of the state of his mind in this letter to one of the confidants of his anguish. "All ties of birth, of blood, of memory, of affection, happiness, interests, all the fascinations which can be exercised over a man's will, attach me to my present belief. To doubt of it is to cast doubts on all that is dear to me. If I had to give this up it would be as death to me."

Happily, there went on in him at the same time a practical work that brought forth fruits in his life, and that was to give him the decisive impulse. The Oxford Movement had given him a fresh conception of the Church, perhaps the notion of unity; but it was faith in the Holy Spirit, in His proper office, in His constant action, in the Church as the source of infallibility, in souls as the cause of certainty—that was ready to complete the work, to re-unite the *membra disjecta* of this doctrine, and make of them a living religion. Nothing is more striking than to discover to what a degree Manning was already a Catholic through instinct, heart, practice, and methods, while he fought this inner battle, and believed himself still an Anglican. He was a Catholic in his conception of the sacraments, in his celebration of the Eucharistic sacrifice, in his practice of confession.

Manning confessed himself, sometimes to his curate Laprimaudaye, who preceded him in entering the Catholic Church, sometimes to other priests.

He received the confessions of the faithful, and taught that the sacrament of penance, far from being a counsel of perfection, as Robert Wilberforce in a moment of laxity had insinuated, was a command all the more strictly obligatory as sin is more abundant. A curious letter from him sets forth to Mrs. Sidney Herbert, wife of the eminent statesman (his particular friend), his views on the delicate subject of the rights of the priest and the husband in the matter of confession and of direction of consciences. Like all Anglo-Catholics of that time, Manning rather violated the rules of the Church while making use of her offices. Confession was carried on at random, without much heed to the limits of the parish and the diocesan's rights. There is a story, but one which irrefutable testimony forbids me to accept, that Manning, when a Catholic archbishop, showed this same grievous disdain for order, and only ceased encroaching upon other bishops' territory, in his confessions and office as director, after having been forcibly remonstrated with.

Still, he had somewhat strained the wise practice of the Church, by giving from the pulpit in sermons addressed to all, precepts and instructions on conduct that the true director of consciences takes care to model according to the natures and dispositions of his penitents. Mr. Gladstone, who wittily begged his friend to open " the compartment of casuistry," with which Manning's mind as well as his own was provided, in order to discuss some striking case of conscience, justly represented to him that, according to the rules of life laid down in one of his sermons, a Member of Parliament, a Minister, like himself, would be obliged to give up his career.

Manning was not less severe to himself. Not only in Lent, but at all times, he had fixed hours for prayer, meditation, reading, and self-examination. He fasted, at least on Wednesdays and Fridays. He rigidly followed the practice of reading the Bible and of repeating the Penitential Psalms, kneeling. He mortified his flesh by special forms of abstinence. For instance, after 1847 he gave up the luxury of horses and carriages. These were the beginnings of that asceticism that he was afterwards to carry to such an extent. This mode of living is hardly in the Protestant spirit. Manning also showed it by his use of certain formulas and expressions of the purest Catholicism; he spoke of the altar, of the sacrifice; he promised his friends to commemorate them *in sacro;* he wrote his private and confidential letters *sub sigillo confessionis.* Mr. Purcell, who takes pleasure in noticing trifles, remarks that in 1847 Manning, while using a vocabulary impregnated with Catholicism, was still ignorant of the quasi-technical terms of Catholic devotion, and wrongly designated the

Sacred Heart and the Benediction of the Blessed Sacrament. This simply proves to what an extent this inner development was spontaneous and personal.

In spite of his continuous progress in this path, Manning did not find calmness and joy. During these years, when he was called upon to play a prominent part in the metropolis and the Church, he accused himself of worldliness and ambition, of human aims and cowardly compromises. This self-styled ambitious man was none the less deeply disturbed by the offer of the post of Sub-Almoner to the Queen, vacant through the promotion of his brother-in-law, Samuel Wilberforce, to the Episcopate. This was the first step in the ladder of honours. He refused it, after having thoroughly sounded his conscience and minutely examined his motives. He showed himself, indeed, the same man who thanked God for having spared him the temptation of becoming a bishop; this he did on hearing of the preferment to the Episcopate of a friend, who by his acceptance betrayed the cause of Truth which up till then he had professed, and remained an Anglican by accepting consecration.

God led him indeed by other ways. A serious illness that, in the spring of 1847, compelled him to cease his occupations, and brought him face to face with death, was for him a spiritual renewal. He gave himself up to a minute self-examination;

126

heart but it is quite wrong.

he weighed his motives, his actions, thoughts, even prayers in the scales of holiness, and vowed himself more completely to God. His private journal of this time is a long and mystical communion of his soul with Christ. From this crisis, during which he had also the misfortune to lose his mother, he himself dated his conversion, previously faintly sketched by the evangelical Miss Bevan.

The remarkable part of this development was, that the renewal of Manning's piety and faith was closely connected with his growing conviction of the truth of Catholicism. How could he doubt that the call, which he heard ever urging him more towards Rome, came from Heaven itself, since he felt himself more and more in communion with Christ? He who detested controversy, who, to others walking the same way as himself, had showed the danger of neglecting the means of rudimentary and sufficient grace, in his own Church, in order to seek for a distant ecclesiastical ideal, finally decided, that for his altered conscience the springs of eternal life gushed forth at the feet of St. Peter's Chair and of the Vicar of Christ. Henceforth his Catholicism was no longer a temptation, it was a religion; it was no longer a theory, it was a reality, and the whole soul, not only the reason or the mind, received its imprint.

At the end of this long retirement, during which it seemed to him that God weaned him from everything, in order to fill him entirely with Himself and to become his only possession, his doctors sent him to the Continent. There he spent the summer of 1847, and the first six months of 1848, especially at Rome. This journey was properly speaking a course of ecclesiology and practical Catholicism. Manning obeyed the principles of the Oxford School in going to the Catholic churches on the Continent. The Tractarians, faithful to the theory that Anglicanism was a branch of the Universal Church, would have thought it equally wrong to attend Catholic chapels in England and not to attend churches of that form of worship in France and Italy. Nevertheless, the practice scarcely corresponded to the theory. When Newman was converted, he had never spoken to more than two Catholic priests. Oakeley, having by chance entered a Catholic chapel, had fled precipitately, conscience-stricken. Manning had none of these scruples. He was assiduous in attending all the services, conversed with all the priests, visited all the monasteries. The rites of this form of worship strengthened him in his inner Catholicism. These symbolical acts, this objective religion, the great drama of expiation and salvation, ever being renewed and yet ever the same, all these things seemed to him to make the great realities of the faith more evident. In his eyes, the Protestant worship was hardly worthy of the name; sometimes, as in the Cathedral of Basle, where he stopped in his journey, it offered not austere simplicity, but the dryness and bareness of cold rationalism; sometimes, as in the English churches, it presented to the faithful the soulless body, the imitation of the forms, without the vivifying dogma of Catholicism. But in St. Peter's, in the Cathedral of Liège, in the Basilica of Aix-la-Chapelle, in the *Portioncula* of Assisi, he felt at ease, at home, in intimate communion with .the service and the priest.

At Rome, he breathed the air of the Catholic metropolis freely. To occupy his leisure, he saw the beginning of Pius IX.'s career and of a revo-lution. He conversed with men of the various parties, with Father Ventura and other monks. The sovereign Pontiff granted him two audiences, on April 9 and May 11, the day of his departure. His diary of that time, so copious upon all else, mentions this fact in two lines. Happily the Cardinal filled in the omissions of the Anglican. Pius IX., to whom he presented a report on the Irish famine, from his friend, Sidney Herbert, spoke to him of Mrs. Fry, the prison-reformer; this introduced the subject of Quakers; he then turned to the English Church, the ob-servance of Sundays and Saints' Days, the Com-munion in both kinds. Finally he praised the good works which abounded in England, adding this somewhat Pelagian remark—"When men perform good works, God gives His grace;" turning his eyes towards Heaven, he ended with these words—"My poor prayers are daily offered for England." Thus ended this memorable interview between two men destined to exercise together so great an influence over the Church and the age.

However, hardly had he returned to England, than Manning plunged again into the thick of the strife. He found the Anglican world a prey to violent agitation. Hampden, whose appointment to the Chair of Theology at Oxford had already provoked a serious crisis, had just been made a bishop. Manning had in his letters violently condemned this choice. He surprised and scandalized some of his friends by the language of his Charge. In it he adopted the method of having recourse to a purely formal expedient, and refusing, until fresh orders, to regard as a heretic a man whom the Church had not officially stamped with that designation. Mr. Purcell looks upon this action, which is indeed difficult to explain, as a fresh example of the supple diplomacy of Manning. It may well be that the indefinite prolongation of this impossible dualism between Catholic convictions and the Anglican position of the Archdeacon of Chichester had exercised a demoralizing influence upon him. Perhaps, however, we must see in it only a legal scruple, and the very natural repugnance of a man, in whose eyes the whole of the English Established Church was scarcely more than a gigantic fiction, to make a scapegoat of an unfortunate prelate. Nevertheless, this situation had its perils. Manning was in a measure cut in half. He was naturally exposed to self-contradiction; when troubled souls turned to him, as formerly to Newman, to lead them back to the English fold, his embarrassment was great. To confide to them his own doubts, to admit them to his inner struggles, would have gone beyond his rights and violated his secret. Forced to detain them provisionally in the Church to which he still belonged, he was induced to use arguments of which he did not feel sure, and when he had succeeded, it was sometimes too thoroughly, and in spite of his ulterior efforts he found he had for ever turned away a soul from the truth to which he later yielded submission. Sometimes, however, truth had its way, in spite of prudence, as when he replied to a young Anglican who consulted him on the practical obligations of a purely Catholic soul— " The place of a man who believes all the dogmas of the Catholic Church is in that Church."

Nevertheless, for a man like Manning, action is in itself such a virtue, such a temptation, such an intoxication, that he sometimes forgot, in the warmth of public speech or of a private con-

versation, not only his most deeply-seated convictions (that was serious enough), but, what was
still worse, the spiritual realities on which they
were founded.   Another danger arose from his
practising approximation for ritual devotion and
asceticism, so that he ran the risk of blunting religious sensitiveness, and of falling into that kind of
clerical dilettanteism which the Anglican ritualism
has sometimes become.   I say this without wishing
in the least to attack the serious intentions and the
fidelity of men who courageously follow their own
consciences : the effects of Catholicism will not be
felt by those who merely play at it.   A clergy
without vocation, an unconsecrated service, an
illegitimate authority, an unreal religion, all these
are only the husk.   The kernel is not there, and
the soul runs the risk of wearing itself out by
contact with these empty forms.

A nature famishing for reality, action, truth, as
Manning's, could not for ever be satisfied with
the unsubstantial food of Anglo-Catholicism.   He
began to feel that the very truths he possessed,
the half-certainties that kept him in the Established
Church, called for complementary certainties, and
that if he did not continue to the end he would
lose the little he had.   In his eyes Christianity
implied Catholicism ; systematically to reject the
latter would be to place himself voluntarily outside
the former.   In other words, for him, as previously

for Newman, the question of his soul's salvation began to gain precedence over that of consistent doctrine and coherent convictions. The purely intellectual problem disappeared; the religious, moral, vital problem brought itself more and more clearly forward. Manning could no longer give to himself or to others the advice to cling humbly to the certainties shared by all Churches, to practise simply the virtues that belong equally to Catholicism and Protestantism, to ask only for those rudimentary graces that are the common patrimony of all sincere souls. He could no longer repeat that this was not a vital question, and that it was lawful for him to wait for a more decided call from on high. The inner work was complete; the circle was described; external events were about to give the final impetus.

I have described at such length this psychological development, not only on account of the interest afforded by the history of a soul, and of such a soul! but especially to reply to the allegations of Mr. Purcell and some of his critics, who have either seen, or wished to see, a course of action taken purely from party policy, in Manning's tardy conversion, in this conversion, that was truly the outcome of a ceaseless spiritual struggle during six years, and the slowly-ripened fruit of a wonderful development of piety. If the explanation that I have given is not a sufficient refutation of this foolish calumny, if there does not issue from it the wearied, but bright and beneficent countenance of one of the masters of the spiritual life struggling with the terrible problem of authority, I shall have written in vain. Not that I think of contesting the influence upon Manning's final resolution of such incidents as the famous judgment in the Gorham case. All that I assert, is that for Manning, as for Newman, the final impetus did but determine an act long prepared for by a purely inner development.

The Rev. G. Gorham was a clergyman who was ordained in 1811; that is to say, at a time of disciplinary and doctrinal laxity. The Bishop of Exeter made no difficulty the first time in instituting him to a living, but when Gorham wished, later, to make an exchange, the same prelate refused, on account of Gorham's views on, or rather against, Baptismal Regeneration. Gorham appealed to the Court of Arches, the ecclesiastical Court of the Province of Canterbury. Defeated there, he carried his appeal before the Judicial Committee of the Privy Council, that is to say, before the Final Court of Appeal in English law. It was a purely lay court, since it was the Queen, in her quality as Head of the State, and consequently, according to the Protestant theory of the *summus episcopus*, as Head of the Church, who there administered justice. The presence of three prelates, with purely consultative rights, made no change, especially as they were in a minority. This Court pronounced in favour of the Rev. G. Gorham. The judgment brought out two facts with the greatest clearness. The first was the Royal Supremacy, a well-known fact. From the time of Henry VIII. and Elizabeth, this fact had been the foundation of the English Reformation and the Established Church. Usually, it was discreetly concealed. It had been tacitly ignored by the Anglo-Catholic reaction. Men spoke of the Universal Church, of Councils, of the rule of faith ; they systematically forgot that all these fine things were pure theory, and that in fact what the English Church believed and professed, and had to believe and profess, was what Henry VIII. had willed, what Elizabeth had instituted, what Victoria maintained. The judgment of the Privy Council was a recall to reality.

The second fact was that this usurpation by the State, which had become the supreme judge of doctrine, was now no longer a judicial fiction. It was this time exercised against Episcopal authority, and in favour of a definite heresy. Not only was the Church harshly warned that she was not mistress of herself, of her faith, of her discipline, but the true master declared that all that had been said, written, preached for the past seventeen years, the whole of Anglo-Catholicism in fact, was a lie. It was allowable for an English clergyman, for a priest, as the Tractarians said, to deny a sacrament, to teach and practise Calvinism, even pure Zwinglianism.

This was too much for minds filled with Neo-Catholicism, and their excitement was great. It was no longer a question of knowing, as in 1845, whether the premises laid down by Newman permitted men to refuse obedience to the seat of unity, to Rome. The question was whether, for the safety of one's soul, one could remain in a Church that had become a purely human institution, whose faith, creeds, sacraments, discipline, appointments, were at the mercy of the lay tribunals that sat in the name of civil sovereignty. Mr. Gladstone rose from a sick-bed to tell Manning: " The English Church is lost if she does not save herself by an act of courage." At the last moment, the statesman drew back before his own temerity. At a meeting held at his house he refused to sign his name—on account of his oath as Privy Councillor—to the protest, drawn up by Manning and signed by twelve of the faithful, some of them priests, among whom were Manning the Archdeacon, Robert Wilberforce, Pusey, Mill the Cambridge Professor of Hebrew, Henry Wilberforce, Keble, and Hope Scott.

On March 19, 1850, in the cathedral library at Chichester, Manning presided over a meeting of the clergy of his archdeaconry, who adopted a shorter but no less clear formula of protest. He drew up a declaration against the Royal Supremacy, and had it signed by 1800 members of the clergy. Then, before taking the final resolutions, perhaps in expectation, against all probability, of a favourable solution at the eleventh hour, he shut himself up in retirement. It was, but five years later, his Littlemore, the death-struggle of his Anglicanism. It lasted nine months, from March to December, 1850. As he wrote to Robert Wilberforce, "each morning, on opening his eyes, his heart almost broke : he felt himself torn to pieces between truth and affection." Anglicanism, in his eyes, was "a mere ruin." Sometimes he caught clear glimpses of the port to which he was bound, " Rome, centre of the One, Holy, Visible, Infallible Church." At other times, vague visions floated before his eyes. " If I remain an Anglican, I shall end by being a mere mystic. God is a Spirit; He has no visible kingdom, no Church, no sacraments. Nothing, in any case, will make me return to English Protestantism nor to any other."

He opened his heart freely to Robert Wilberforce, who was going through the same crisis. With regard to the public, to those even of his friends who, like Gladstone, could not conceive the sacrilegious idea of leaving the National Church, he thought he ought to be silent so long as his decision had not been irrevocably taken. Perhaps he still hoped vaguely against all hope that the archbishops, in their position as spiritual heads, as

Patriarchs of the English Church, would intervene to re-establish the purity of the faith. He had to renounce this simple illusion when he saw the Archbishop of Canterbury, Sumner, refuse to receive a deputation, refrain, together with all the bishops except four, from joining in the debate upon the Bill brought in by the Bishop of London for transferring to the Episcopal body the ecclesiastical jurisdiction from the Court of Appeal of the Privy Council, and moreover declare that he would never dispute the sentence of a regular tribunal, and that he saw nothing illegal in the admission to the cure of souls of a clergyman opposed to Baptismal Regeneration. This was not quite the attitude of the Apostles, proudly declaring to the Sanhedrim that it was better to obey God than men. Thus the Church was not only reduced to slavery, but she was thus reduced with the express consent of her chiefs, who betrayed her. All that remained to her was the name of Church; the reality had disappeared.

All Manning's friends, his brother-in-law, Samuel Wilberforce, Bishop of Oxford, whose two brothers were passing through the same crisis, Gladstone, Pusey, his relations, his eldest brother, who wrote to him letters blaming his conduct, and who always refused to see him after his conversion;—all felt truly that it was over, that the submission to Rome of the Rector of Lavington was merely an affair of

weeks, almost of days. Mr. Purcell, forgetting the
documents that he has himself published, tries
again to convict him of duplicity. Manning per-
formed, no doubt, the strictest duties of his office,
but his heart was at Rome. On November 17, he
was obliged to convoke and to preside at a meeting
of the clergy of his archdeaconry to protest against
the Papal bull which, much to the anger of the
State Church and of popular Protestantism, had
just restored the Catholic hierarchy, suppressed in
England since Elizabeth's accession. It was an
extraordinarily false position; he felt this, and he
took this opportunity to communicate to his brethren in the ministry the state of his mind, and his
formal resolution to quit the English Church.

The hour of final hesitation, of last struggles,
was over. Manning had not yielded to haste nor
to passion; he had fought as long as he dared
against the voice of conscience: longer perhaps
than a less scrupulous soul would have done.

By degrees, he had untied all the bonds that had
connected him with that deeply-loved, faithfully-
served Church. He had passed this time of retirement in reading the breviary, in an initiation into
the spiritual beauties of the liturgy that had calmed
his soul. For the last time he went to kneel by
Mr. Gladstone's side in an English Church, in
Buckingham Palace Road, in which preached an
Anglican clergyman destined to become a father of

the Society of Jesus. When the Communion Service began, Manning rose, saying to his saddened companion—"I can no longer communicate in the Church of England." On April 6, 1851, the fifth Sunday in Lent, Manning and his friend Hope Scott, who had promised to bear each other company, abjured, confessed, made their profession of faith, and received conditional Baptism and Absolution from the hands of the Rev. Father Brown-Hill, at the church in Hill Street. The doubts that had tortured him until "the opening of Father Brown-Hill's door" disappeared as by magic. The following Sunday (Palm Sunday) Cardinal Wiseman confirmed them, and gave them the Communion in his private chapel.

It was the end of a life. Manning believed that it was even the end of his life, or at least of all public activity for him. He had, indeed, unhesitatingly resolved to be ordained a priest, but there his ideas had stopped; he thought he should live and die in quiet obscurity, in the shadow of the sanctuary. At last, after so many storms, he had found peace, as is proved by this letter—"I feel that I have no other desire than to persevere in what God has given me for the sake of His Son. What a blessed ending! As the soul says to Dante— *E de martirio venni a questa pace!*"

The *Times*, in 1852, having believed itself authorized to announce his return to Anglicanism,

140

received the following from him—"I have found in the Catholic Church all that I sought, more even than I should have been capable of imagining, so long as I remained outside her." Manning was not one of those who turn back, nor of those who, once they have known and embraced the truth, fall asleep in cowardly and selfish idleness.

CATHOLIC YEARS

I

AT the age of forty-four, after having been a clergyman for eighteen years and a dignitary of the English Church for eleven, Manning found himself alone, outside the pale, cast off, without occupation or friends, almost without connections. In these sad experiences, he thought he saw a warning of God against human attachments; he set himself on the watch against exclusive affections. It was certainly not that the springs of love had dried up in that soul, whence we shall see them gush forth freely enough until the close of his life. Freed from purely human and earthly affections, he had not yet found in the practice of heroic, almost superhuman charity, a use for his power of loving. His predominant feeling was joy, heavenly joy, the gladness of a soul at last supported by a full flood of grace.

He had never hesitated for a moment in following his priestly vocation. Less than ten weeks after his abjuration, on the eve of Trinity Sunday,

Cardinal Wiseman ordained him in his private chapel, and two days after, on Monday, June 16, Manning, quickly initiated by Father Faber, of the Oratory, into that ceremonial which, according to some unkindly critics, he never thoroughly knew, celebrated his first mass at the Jesuit Church, with Father de Ravignan as his assistant. Although the Cardinal already had views for him, he agreed to his going to study in Rome. Pius IX. welcomed him there with these words that came from the heart: *Vi benedico con tutto il mio cuore in tuo egressu et in tuo ingressu*, treated him as a son, invited him to a friendly conversation once a month, and placed him at the *Academia dei nobili ecclesiastici*.

Mortifying as it must have been for a man of his age to go back to school, to return, as he said, to the seminarist's bib and leading-strings, as St. Ignatius had done before him, this sojourn at Rome left a bright streak in his life. Outside his studies and the privilege of his intercourse with the Pope, he became intimate with the chief personages of the Curia, of the Tesus, with Father-General Beckx, the great theologian Perrone, Father Passaglia, who read with him the *Summa* of St. Thomas Aquinas. After three years, Pius IX., who would have gladly kept him near to himself, had to yield him to the repeated entreaties of Cardinal Wiseman.

The Cardinal-Archbishop, by summoning him to his aid, justly recognized the demands of the situation. English Catholicism was passing through a great crisis. The object during more than two centuries of a persecution, sometimes bloody, constantly harassing, it had furnished numberless martyrs to Protestant intolerance, in the persons of its priests, heroic rebels to the religion of Henry VIII. and Elizabeth, or of its laymen, given over as victims of the Catholic Plot, to the monstrous lies of a Titus Oates. It had endured not only those sufferings that bring with them compensation to lofty souls. Through its civil and political disabilities, it had experienced the most cruel part of persecution, that contraction of mind and heart eventually produced in its victims. A revocation of the Edict of Nantes, or the terror of a Revolution, plucks the flower of a nation, throws it outside, or coops it up inside in a sort of home-exile, turning choice spirits into a coterie infected with the spirit of the *Refuge* or of *Emigration*.

English Catholicism did not escape this law. Its priests were the chaplains of some noble families. The laity were, like the French Legitimists, in the position of emigrants in their own land. There was no middle class. The poorer people were mainly Irish emigrants. In London, the aristocracy attended the chapels of the Catholic Embassies and Legations; the poor districts had only humble mission-halls. Elsewhere it was still worse. At Liverpool, there were four chapels and fourteen priests for more than 100,000 faithful. Four great events, that marked in a fashion the stages of a long evolution, changed the aspect of affairs.

The French Revolution, by suppressing the Colleges of Douai and Saint-Omer, forced back to their native soil the young clergy preparing for the priesthood; at the same time as Protestant and insular prejudices were weakened by the dignified example of the French priests among the *émigrés*, and by the new-born feeling of the unity of Churches and aristocracies against the powers of destruction. The Irish Catholic Emancipation in 1828, the stormy invasion of O'Connell and his *barbarians*, that is to say, of the democracy and its doings, into the peaceful sheepfold, where the *little flock* had, until then, browsed, without straying, on rather tasteless herbage, inaugurated a new era. There was henceforth an English Catholicism that would not put up with the disdainful toleration granted to an inoffensive minority; it was conscious of the grandeur and the force of its principle; it carried war into the camp of authorized Anglicanism or of militant Protestantism. Wiseman was its leader and champion. At the same time, the Oxford Movement, by once again raising the place of Catholicism in the English Church, and by throwing into the Catholic Church Newman, Faber, Ward, Oakeley, Dalgairns, Coffin, Manning, and many others, changed the moral atmosphere. A land struck with barrenness for three centuries bore new harvests, a dried-up stem began again to flower. The Church, once more a conqueror, raised her head. The new-comers, excited by the struggle, had not debased their courage in cowardly idleness. They showed no signs of foreign taint, they gave forth no uncertain tone. They did not believe that the conquest of the truth, at the cost of most painful sacrifices, ought to exclude them from the arena of noble combats.

There was henceforth in English Catholicism two divisions, two classes, two parties: the timid and the valiant, the dumb and the eloquent, the passive and the active, the Old and the New Catholics. If this division did not always correspond to the origins, if there were Catholics of the old stock amongst the zealots, and, amongst the moderates, new converts, one especially, the greatest of all, this classification was none the less exact as a whole. It was natural that the ex-Protestants should be fascinated in their new Church by all they had lacked in the old; a present and visible authority, a living Infallibility, an alert and joyous obedience. If all did not go as far as Ward (who would have liked to receive every day at breakfast-time with his morning paper a Pontifical Encyclical with dogmatic definitions), all were, at least by vocation, what men have agreed to call Ultramontanes. A conflict was inevitable with the semi-Gallicanism and the timid reserve of Catholics by birth.

Pius IX. hastened it by re-establishing the ecclesiastical hierarchy, and by substituting for the Apostolic Vicariates an Archbishopric and twelve Bishoprics. By proclaiming England ripe for a return to the normal organism of ecclesiastical life, the Apostolic Letters *Universalis Ecclesiæ* repudiated at the same time the chimerical hope of seeing the English Church as a body, its clergy headed by its prelates, submit to the Vicar of Jesus Christ. This act provoked an explosion of Protestant fanaticism, with which Lord John Russell associated himself by an Act passed *ab irato*, which was tacitly repealed before even being put in force, an Act to forbid Catholic bishops the use of territorial titles. In the Church itself the offensive movement of propaganda and conquest received a great impetus. The Holy See had a devoted officer in Wiseman, created a Cardinal and Archbishop. Unhappily, the Episcopate included too many members filled with the old spirit, for perfect unity to prevail amongst those in command.

The ten years that passed between Manning's return to London and his accession to the Archiepiscopal throne, were full of sad struggles between

the two opposing principles, still further complicated with deplorable personal questions. Manning
was forced to take part in them through the nature
of his opinions, through his temperament, and
above all, through the confidence placed in him
by his Archbishop.

From the beginning he had, as an act of obedience, to found a community of Oblates, and this
made him many enemies. Cardinal Wiseman com-
plained of not finding, on account of the insufficient number of his clergy, the help that he desired
amongst the regulars of his diocese. The quarrel
between diocesan authority and the Orders went
far back in English history. Had not Saint-Cyran,
under the name of Petrus Aurelius, interfered in
it already? Manning's ideal, as was proved by
his foundation of the Congregation of the diocesan
missionary priests of the Oblates of St. Charles,
was not that of the Orders, devoted to the perfection of the inner and contemplative religious
life, not even when this was modified by the large
concessions made to practical and external life by
the Institute of Ignatius Loyola,—it was that of
communities of secular priests living under rule
and as a society, but with a view to serving as
a reserve, and, if the term may be used, as *central
brigades* for the head of the diocese.

It was to this foundation that he turned without
delay. Wiseman, who had successfully employed

him during the Crimean War, in negotiating with the Government for a Catholic Chaplain to the army, independent of the English Chaplain-general, could not yet place him over a parish. He desired him to form this band of auxiliaries, the need for which was all the more pressing since it was useless, as he wrote with some bitterness to Father Faber, to appeal to existing Orders. Manning studied at San Sepolcro, near Milan, the model institute of St. Charles Borromeo, and submitted to Rome the project he had elaborated. It was approved by Cardinal Barnabo, head of the Congregation of the Propaganda which dealt with English affairs. The Pope gave his special blessing and sanction to the statutes, January 21, 1857.

Three principal points formed the essence of this rule of life: strict submission of the community to the head of the diocese, a number of spiritual exercises and theological studies fixed and calculated to keep up to a certain level the spirit of this institution; lastly, the purely secular nature of the society, mingling with the clergy of the diocese, joining in their works. Manning loved to bring forward, with regard to this foundation, the immense riches of Catholicism. For Catholicism includes the religious life of the cloisters, the practice of the counsel of perfection of the Gospel, with its many varieties, from pure contemplation and adoration to the manual or intellectual labour

149

of the Benedictines, even to the almost complete suppression of choral services, and the strict sub-ordination of the exercises of worship to external activity, as in the Society of Jesus. It possesses those communities of priests, those brotherhoods without vows, intermediate between the isolation of the secular clergy and the stationary com-munity-life of the Orders. Finally, it makes use of the most wonderful instrument of propa-ganda, of moral influence, and of hierarchical obedience in the persons of the secular clergy and the simple priest, that cornerstone of the whole edifice. What strength in that infinite variety! What knowledge of the spiritual keyboard and its numberless keys! How one understands the fact that Protestantism, even when most faithful to the spirit of the Reformation, has sometimes a tend-ency to borrow or to imitate these valuable means of action!

On Whitsunday, 1857, Manning was able to inaugurate his Institute. Five priests and two clerics—that was the whole of the effective force —were installed at Bayswater. The next day, at five o'clock in the morning, they celebrated Mass in a neighbouring church, still in course of con-struction. Two thousand Catholics living in the district, an unfinished church where Mass was said on Sundays and once in the week, a school with forty poor children,—such were the beginnings of this work. For eight years Manning presided over his community of the Oblates of St. Charles. There he met with cruel trials, fought many tough battles, endured severe defeats; but he wrote in 1875: "The eight years at St. Mary's have been the happiest in my life." His name remains inscribed over the door of the little room where the Cardinal Archbishop of Westminster loved sometimes to retire, that he might again taste the delights of peace.

Peace! yet it was not peace that marked this phase of his existence. Along with the untiring activity that he displayed, he had to fight ceaseless battles. Even his dear community of Oblates of St. Charles brought violent attacks upon him. In the absence of regular seminaries, Cardinal Wiseman entrusted him with the direction of St. Edmund's College, where the Westminster and Southwark clergy were trained. He had not consulted the head of the latter diocese—Monsignor Grant— formerly his intimate friend, now his persistent opponent. This prelate gained from the Westminster Chapter a protest, as vehement as his own, took the matter to the Vatican, and won his cause on the ground of some formal error. Wiseman had to submit to this decree. The interference of the Westminster Chapter was the first symptom of an opposition that gave way only in the long run. For the moment, Manning suffered the

penalty for the earlier favours of Pius IX. When—
April 8, 1857, six years to a day since his abjuration—he was made Provost or Dean of the Westminster Chapter, this rapid promotion, unexpected
by him as well as by his new colleagues, carried
their irritation to its height.

Though raised to an important position in the
hierarchy, Manning was about to enter on a struggle
against violent hatreds. He saw in Wiseman the
direct representative of the Holy See, and thought
himself happy in sharing, like the majority of the
new converts, the Cardinal's Ultramontane doctrines.
He was convinced that the opposition he met with
was animated by an anti-Roman and anti-papal
spirit, and that there would be no safety for English
Catholicism until the present generation of bishops
infected with Gallicanism had passed away, and he
remained the Cardinal's right hand in the painful
strife that filled the last years of his Episcopate.
Wiseman had not many helpers in those about him.
The isolation of this great servant of the Church, in
his last days, is truly pathetic. His most intimate
companion, the man to whom in the gradual decay
of his health and his want of experience in business
matters, he entrusted the care of his temporal
interests, Monsignor Searle, lacked delicacy and
true affection, and was devoted to the Old Catholic
party. This deplorable situation was partly the cause
of the serious mistake that embittered his last days.

Wiseman let himself be persuaded that he needed a coadjutor, and allowed himself to be over-influenced in the choice he made, a choice all the more important as its object should be invested with the right of succession. Choice fell upon Monsignor Errington, Bishop of Plymouth from 1851 to 1856, and made on this occasion titular Archbishop of Trebizond. Scarcely had this alliance been formed, that decided incompatibility of temper was revealed between Cardinal Wiseman, ardent, bold, a friend to generous undertakings, a patron of the New Catholics, and approving their conquering zeal as neophytes, and Monsignor Errington, a scion of an old race, as proud of the spotlessness of their coat-of-arms as of that of their faith. Daily contact — they lived together — the excitements of party spirit, were not long in turning this primary want of sympathy into violent antipathy.

The tragic part of this position lay in its apparent hopelessness. Was Wiseman, as he grew older, to allow his authority gradually to slip into the hands of Searle and Errington? If he had not possessed at that time a confidant, an energetic adviser, he would have continued to groan over the evil without trying to remedy it. Manning in this crisis was the support, perhaps the inspiration, of the Cardinal.

In his opinion, it was a question of a great and

decisive battle between error and truth, between consistent, logical Catholicism, faithful to its principles, and a spurious, emasculated Catholicism, adapted to the world and to the age. For such a man as he, it was a sacred duty to lend a helping hand to the cause of the Holy See and of unalloyed religion, compromised by the feeble health of a prelate. The future of the Church in England depended upon it. The question was whether Wiseman's successor would continue, or whether he would destroy the other's work, whether he would appeal to the new forces, or whether he would return to the anti-Roman, anti-papal, anti-Catholic Catholicism of former days. As Procurator of the Cardinal, Manning negotiated for him at the Vatican. He kept up an assiduous correspondence with the Chamberlain of Pius IX., Monsignor George Talbot, who had the Pope's ear, whom a similarity of destiny and convictions had brought into intimacy with Manning, and who acted as an intermediary between the Sovereign Pontiff and those of his friends in England who wished to dispense with the official intermediary action of the Propaganda.

If Manning made greater use than any one else of this means, Wiseman, who had appointed him his Procurator, had nothing but praise to give to his zeal. While the Cardinal, by means of fine petitions written in excellent style, was making rather feeble attempts to procure the revocation of his coadjutor's appointment, Manning worked at it from 1859. Appointed Apostolic Protonotary, with the title of Monsignor, in the following year, he took his place in that very special body of men who help the Pope in his government of the Church. In England, the crisis became worse; almost all the bishops took part with Errington; the secondary clergy gave themselves up to indecent controversies, even in the Protestant and Liberal newspapers; all the laity took the side of the champion of hereditary Catholicism, of saintly somnolence, and of *dolce far niente*.

It was the moment for dangerous compromises. Wiseman, through lassitude, was only too much inclined to them. Freed since 1861, by a Pontifical Act, from the presence of a coadjutor who had become odious to him, he attached the less importance to the question of the right of succession to his office, upon which all turned, and which in reality, and in Manning's opinion, was the most important of all. Thus it was the Procurator who would have no compromise on this matter. To the dark prophecies of schism uttered by Cardinal Barnabo, Prefect of the Propaganda, he replied by a full confidence in the effect of an act of authority. Let Rome speak, said he, and all will go well. He wrote—" I have the calm conviction that this is one of those *causae majores* in which the Holy See is especially guided by our Lord, who is specially present." Such certainty is indeed faith, it has the same moral quality, it gives out the same full, pure sound. Therefore, in Manning, that Ultramontanism with which he has been so keenly reproached, very far from belonging to the domain of politics, even ecclesiastical politics, or anything appertaining to them, was the very fruit of his piety, his slowly elaborated convictions, and his religious experiences. The man who could write the following lines, intended for the eyes of an intimate friend only, might have been mistaken, but the theories were not adopted to flatter a Sovereign Pontiff on whom his career depended—"The truth, the truth which alone has saved me, is the Infallibility of the Vicar of Jesus Christ, in as far as it is the only and perfect form of the infallibility of the Church, and consequently of all faith, all unity, and all obedience."

It cannot be too often repeated that with him Ultramontanism was only the final term, the logical issue of a development of the inner life and of piety whose other fruits were, unfailing faith, boundless charity, rigorous personal asceticism. Those are truly to be pitied whose eyes are shut through party feeling to this entirely spiritual and religious origin of the truly Roman Catholicism of Manning, or who refuse to see in his particular conception of Christianity the ever-flowing source of that wide love of mankind, and the cause of that bold view of the rights and duties of society, by which the last part of his career was influenced. For we get here to the very core of our subject: let us then make once more the assertion, paradoxical though it may seem, that Manning's Ultramontanism was a form of his piety, a halting-place in his spiritual progress, and that in it he found the inspiration of his Christian socialism, the motive power of his activity for the people, the spring and the regulator of his generous boldness of thought, language, and conduct. It would be absurd to strain a point, and to pretend to draw from this fact general conclusions; but it is a fact that Manning was an Ultramontane in proportion as he was a great Christian, and that he was the apostle of reforming Catholicism and of social reform in proportion as he was an Ultramontane.

In this lies the unity of his life. It is also the message of hope and consolation that he wished to leave to a generation weary of the negations of rationalism, and terrified at the problems of poverty and evil. The plan that gradually formed itself in Manning's mind was that of reconciling the two great opposing currents, by causing them to flow in the same channel, although one current ended in the Vatican Council and the proclamation of the dogma of Infallibility, while the other, after having shaken or overthrown all the postulates of faith and all the principles of certainty, beat its furious waves against the foundations of society itself; to make the Pope, proclaimed and recognized as the incorruptible guardian of the trust of Christian revelation, the Head of a Church that had once more become the refuge of the suffering and the oppressed ; to show to the people, undeceived as to the fictions of *doctrinaire* Liberalism, but crushed under the weight of the realities of economic Liberalism, the incomparable freeing, healing, and regenerating powers of a religion of liberty and authority; in a word, to make of the Gospel of Christ, as interpreted and applied by His Vicar and by the successors of the Apostles, the Charter of humanity; to bring the Church to kneel before the Cross, and the world to kneel before the Church.

He was not deceived, on the whole, in the confidence he had placed in the Holy See. Doubtless, in the course of this six years' struggle, Cardinal Wiseman and his Procurator suffered some defeats. I have already spoken of the matter of St. Edmund's College, where they had to surrender. On the application of a new law relative to the registration of ecclesiastical foundations, Wiseman, who wished to avoid the danger of reviving legislation against property held in mortmain, secured a victory over the majority of the Episcopate. On the other hand, he was over-ruled in the claims he put forward as Metropolitan, with

regard to the inspection of diocesan colleges and
seminaries.

All these differences did not fail to embitter
men's minds. Manning himself was humiliated,
one day, by a violent scene with Monsignor Searle,
that took place not far from Wiseman's sick-bed.
The Cardinal, at times irritated by the systematic
hostility of men as far beneath him in merit, talents,
character, and services as in their hierarchical
position, apologized, by order of the Propaganda,
for some over-keen witticisms. At heart, Cardinal
Barnabo favoured the cause of Errington with that
diplomatic obstinacy whose soft resistance is almost
irresistible. Happily, the Propaganda ended by
declining to pass judgment in so delicate and so
intricate a matter. For it was not a question of
giving a judicial verdict, but of settling an organic
difference. Therefore, although the Holy Office
had declared that there were no canonical grounds
for depriving Monsignor Errington of his *jus successionis*, Pius IX., at last out of patience, having
considered the matter, decided to strike what he
himself called *un colpo di Stato di Dominedio*, and
requested the Archbishop of Trebizond to resign
his rights. Errington obeyed, but he had nevertheless a party in his favour who declared that his
renunciation was null and void, and speculated
upon the re-opening of the question as to who
would succeed Wiseman. To avoid that danger,

there was but one means, viz. the appointment of a new coadjutor *cum jure successionis*. Manning adopted a course that would have resulted in a complete denial of the ambition ascribed to him ; he worked hard in favour of a man who was by no means his friend, Monsignor Ullathorne, Bishop of Birmingham.

Happily this combination met with obstinate, unconquerable resistance : Wiseman had made trial of one coadjutor, he had had enough of him, and at no price would he go through such an experience again. It seemed as if this long struggle had profited Manning but little. It had made for him irreconcilable enemies in the Episcopate, in the clergy, amongst the laity, even in the Protestant and Liberal outside world. He was passing through a painful apprenticeship to unpopularity. As compensation, however, he had gained valuable friendships at Rome. Pius IX., in particular, had seen much of him, had learned to know, to rely on, and to appreciate him. Monsignor George Talbot was devoted to his correspondent. These natural sympathies were to become still warmer by the great services rendered by Manning to the papal cause.

He defended the temporal authority of the Holy See with the same sincerity and passion as he defended its spiritual authority. The mad policy of Napoleon III. had just brought to the front the question of the temporal power in all its gravity.

Italy had constituted itself a State, with the military and political aid of France. Founded in the name of that too famous principle of nationalities, held in honour by the head of the only State that had nothing to expect from it and everything to dread, the young sub-Alpine kingdom only waited champing its bit, before the patrimony of St. Peter, at the veto of the conqueror of Solferino, the sentinel, as it were, of the Vatican. While these contradictions irritated Italians and the partisans of the Legitimist cause alike, average Liberals allowed themselves to believe that the separation of spiritual and temporal power demanded the subjection of the head of a Universal Church to the head of one particular State.

Manning entered the lists by giving a series of lectures, which he issued later in book-form; the zeal displayed in these gained him at first the commendation of the Propaganda, but a little later, it nearly got him into trouble. These lectures were disconcerting by the infinitely more religious than political spirit of their author, the champion of the Holy See. He protested against all comparison of the sacred rights of the Pope with the terrestrial and contingent principle of "Légitimité," and almost condemned the use of material means and recourse to force in order to defend a wholly divine cause.

Non tali auxilio nec defensoribus istis !

This imprudent work was threatened with the Index Expurgatorius. Like Fénelon, Manning was quite ready to submit with a sort of bitter pleasure, "happy, not at having brought himself into the position of incurring this sentence, but of having had the opportunity of giving to his age and his country an example of docility in matters of opinion." He was spared this trial. Some slight formal errors did not prevent either the *Civiltà Cattolica* from speaking favourably of his work, or a new book of his upon the "Glories of the Holy See in the Present Times" from receiving a still warmer welcome.

At this moment occurred the long-expected death of Cardinal Wiseman. Recalled by telegraph from Rome, Manning had the consolation of bidding him farewell before closing his eyes, February 15, 1865. The crisis was all the more serious as great uncertainty prevailed about his successor. Wiseman, cured of his liking for co-adjutors by a single experience, had persistently refused to the end to accept another. There existed a party which supported the indefeasible right of Monsignor Errington, in spite of his renunciation. It was a question of which should prevail —old, sectarian, immovable Catholicism, frightened at its own shadow, or young, ardent, active, aggressive Catholicism. All depended on the choice made by Rome. The Westminster Chapter had to give in the names of three candidates, about whom the bishops were to draw up a confidential report. It seemed certain that if this body avoided offending the Pope by submitting the name of Errington, the dismissed Coadjutor, and if it were well-advised enough to include on its list the name of Ullathorne, Bishop of Birmingham, there would be no difficulty about the choice of that moderate, conciliatory prelate. The Chapter was warned not to send up the name of Errington. It took no notice of the warning, and it committed the most serious fault in not finding room for Monsignor Ullathorne by the side of the Bishops of Clifton and of South-wark, Monsignor Clifford and Monsignor Grant.

From that time the end of the crisis was much more difficult to foresee. The English Government, heretical and schismatical though it was, believed it right to interfere in favour of Grant, who had been favourably looked upon since his disputes with Wiseman. Monsignor Clifford, how-ever, was the favoured candidate. Though he was called somewhat familiarly at Rome *un buon ragazzo*, his birth, connections, temperament secured him the devoted support of all Old Catholicism and of the leaders of the aristocratic laity. Cardinal An-tonelli, a slave to State questions, buried in politics, untouched by spiritual interests, was inclined to pay great attention to the recommendations of the semi-official Britannic agent, Mr. Odo Russell, but

Lord Palmerston's and Lord John Russell's support could not secure the acceptance of the candidateship of Monsignor Grant, of that *piccola testa e pettegola*, as he was called at Rome; of that prelate, spoiled, according to Monsignor Talbot, by seventeen years' sojourn on the banks of the Tiber, which had given him the taste for intrigue and the duplicity of the Italian nature, without its noble fidelity to the Holy See.

All this greatly agitated the capital of Christianity in the spring of 1865. The Cardinals of the Propaganda, Barnabo at their head, scarcely cared to assume the responsibility of an ungrateful task. All depended upon the Pope's decision either to have the matter brought before him, or to let it take its course. An English monk, then at Rome, Father Coffin, openly expressed a wish for what he wittily called, not a " Coup d'Etat," but a *colpo del Spirito Santo*. Monsignor Talbot did not remain inactive. Although Manning had carried his respect for the oath of discretion that he had taken, even so far as to refuse to telegraph to Talbot the names chosen by the Chapter, and though he had discontinued his correspondence with him for three weeks and more at this critical time, from February 24 till March 18, the Chamberlain was kept well enough aware of affairs by the Provost himself, by Patterson and Morris, to be able to counterbalance in the mind of Pius IX. the influence of the agents of Searle, Errington, Grant, Clifford, and Ullathorne. If Talbot intermeddled a little too much, and thought himself more important than he was ; if for an instant he was so delightfully simple as to believe that the Holy Father had cast his eyes upon him, and to convey this to his friend Manning, he was none the less of use in his rank and position.

Rumours were afloat with regard to Manning as a likely choice. He had to undergo those alternations of hope and doubt so cruel to the ambitious. One day, he wrote on the receipt of bad news—" If I were to say that the subject of it has not been before my mind, I should go beyond the truth, but if I say that I have never for a moment believed the thing to be probable, reasonable, or imaginable, I should speak the strict truth. God knows I have never so much as breathed a wish to Him about it. The work, if any, that I have been able to do, does not stand upon the favour or name or countenance of any one under our Lord or His Vicar. If the Holy Father wished our work dissolved, it would be gone before sunset. If he did not, nobody in the world would, I believe, end it. I have offended Protestants, Anglicans, Gallican Catholics, National Catholics, worldly Catholics, and the Government and the public opinion in England, which is running down the Church and the Holy See in all ways and all day long. You are the man who can best

say and know whether this was the way to earthly
reward. In this I hope to go on to the end, and
I know that nothing can take off the edge of the
truth."

No declaration of independence could surpass
in nobility and pride this profession of faith of a
soul that considered obedience as both dignity and
liberty. Manning could firmly await a decision
that might change his destiny, but not his state of
mind.

Pius IX., after hesitating and speaking as if the
choice of Clifford did not depend upon him, had
resolved upon personal intervention; perhaps this
was due to the warmth of resentment caused by
the *insulto al papa* in the nomination of Errington.
He ordered prayers and special Masses to be said
for a month, to invoke help from Heaven. The
answer was not long in coming. The Pope himself said to Manning a few weeks later—" It was
indeed an inspiration which I obeyed in choosing
you. I heard a voice incessantly saying to me,
'Appoint him, appoint him!'" Pius IX. believed
that he dared not resist this divine message. On
April 30, 1865, he appointed Henry Edward
Manning to succeed Cardinal Wiseman as Archbishop of Westminster.

II

ON the morning of May 8, Manning had just said Mass in the chapel of his community of St. Mary of the Angels, Bayswater, when he received the official intimation from the Secretary of the Propaganda. His first impulse was to go and kneel before the Holy Sacrament. He was conscious of the overwhelming responsibilities that he was about to undertake, but he had faith in Him who had willed everything. His first thought was for that part of his new flock who were dearest to his heart, the 20,000 poor children of the Church in London, still outside her help, and whom he hoped to serve. His first actions were naturally marked by the spirit of conciliation; the Archbishop of Westminster could extend his hand to the adversaries of Provost Manning. He was touched by the eagerness shown in congratulating him on his elevation by the very people who had most reason for disliking it. The first priest in the diocese to offer him his congratulations was an opponent, the Capitular Vicar, O'Neal. The Chapter hoped by its deference to make the Archbishop forget six years of violent opposition. Before two days were over, all the Superiors of the Orders, excepting only the Superior of the Jesuits of Farm Street, who sent some fathers in his place, all the heads of parishes, 190 out of 214 priests, came to pay homage to the new Archbishop. The bishops were equally warm in their welcome; Monsignor Ullathorne, whose name had been put forward for succession to this great inheritance, wished to be the first to congratulate his new Metropolitan.

Manning's keenest desire was to be consecrated by the Pope at Rome. He renounced this idea that he might make the service the symbol and pledge of a happy reconciliation. After a retreat at the Convent of the Passionist Fathers at Highgate, he was consecrated on Thursday in Whitsun Week, June 8, 1865, fourteen years after his ordination. The ceremony took place at the Pro-Cathedral, Moorfields; the officiating bishop was Monsignor Ullathorne of Birmingham, assisted by Bishops Grant of Southwark and Clifford of Clifton. Three hundred priests crowded into the nave. When the procession entered with the new Archbishop, his thin figure, his pale, almost transparent face, still further emaciated by rigorous fasting, made an old Irishwoman in the crowd exclaim—

"What a pity to take all this trouble for three weeks!"

But the end was not so near. Manning, who heard this remark, calculated that he might still have fifteen years of activity, but God gave him more than twenty-five. Father Vaughan, his friend and successor, wrote to him that the burden could not well be heavier, but that discouragement could not come to the *Apostle of the Holy Ghost* in England. Wiseman finished his work some years before his death. Manning's was to be, in the mind of his correspondent, at once more ecclesiastical and more spiritual. He was to give England his St. Charles Borromeo and his St. Bartholomew of the Martyrs. Manning felt himself very strong with his motto *sentire cum Petro*, and Pius IX. gave him at Rome, in September, the pallium with his paternal advice, recommending him to be prudent.

There was nothing official in the relations between these two men. Pius IX. tenderly loved the Archbishop, called him the man of Providence, begged him to spare himself, and to imitate that American prelate who adopted the rule of never doing anything that a mere priest could do instead. As to Manning, apart from his convictions on the dogma of Infallibility, he felt personal attachment to the Pope, mingled with veneration. Monsignor Talbot having written to him—"The Holy Father is a very good man, but, as I told you, he is not a saint, he has his weaknesses," Manning, who called Pius IX. the most supernatural being he had ever known, replied—" It is my opinion that the Pope is a saint, and that the *miserie umane* that we find in him existed quite as much in St. Vincent Ferrier." If this view was somewhat exaggerated, there was no flattery in it. Manning's Ultramontanism was no borrowed doctrine, adopted to stand well at court; it was the product, not of mere intellectual work, but of a slow development of the conscience. It was at the very foot of the rock of St. Peter, of that rock on which Christ Himself had said that He would found His Church, that had gushed forth the springs of certainty, of joy, and of life for that soul long tossed on the troubled waves of Protestantism. It remains for me to show, when retracing the episcopal career of Manning, how this Ultramontanism, this absolute and rigorous Catholicism, has been the royal road by which this precursor of a great movement met modern humanity, its needs, its sufferings, and offered it the everlasting Gospel as its only efficacious remedy. With him, breadth of action was in proportion to what his adversaries called narrowness of doctrine. His example showed the error of those who wish to lower and lessen Christianity, to despoil it of its supernatural elements, to make it agree with the spirit of the age. The religion that he believed to be the true one for a sceptical, morbid generation, overwhelmed yet fascinated by its malady, on the watch against the panaceas of quacks, turning away from the pompous and deceitful promises of all-powerful science, but accustomed to the severe methods of science and criticism, is not a Christianity debased, and lowered to the level of a human system of morals or of philosophy; it is the Christianity of the Apostles and Saints; the foolishness of the Cross, the scandal of the Gospel, with its revelation and miracles; the Church, mistress of faith and vanquisher of errors. For Manning, the Catholicism that offers a refuge and a harbour to a generation tossed on a shoreless and bottomless ocean, weary of all and especially of itself, is not a mitigated, sweetened Catholicism, adopted and corrected *ad usum Delphini*, reduced to the sonorous inanities of the *Génie du Christianisme*, ready for every compromise with the State or with reason; it is rather the Catholicism of the great Popes and great monks; the Catholicism of unity, authority, infallibility; the Catholicism of Joseph de Maistre and of the earlier Lamennais. Humanity, according to a finely-expressed thought, is satisfied only with what surpasses it; bows down only before what authoritatively commands. It has never been the method of Christianity to convince by addressing the reason alone. Men must rise above the region of clouds and doubts, of divisions, misunderstanding, and storms, to climb to the summits of faith and divine certainties, to reach the zone of pure springs and wide horizons. Manning detested that deceitful breadth of views which, under pretext of giving easier access to the city of God, destroys its ramparts and delivers its gates into the enemy's hand. In his opinion, sacred narrowness and attachment to unpopular causes are sometimes the very conditions of true breadth.

Such was the real cause of the species of dualism that we think can be traced in his episcopal career. There has been no contradiction between the parts; especially nothing that resembles the diplomacy of a Churchman trying to atone for his excessive devotion to the Papacy by his exaggerated advances to the hardworking democracy. Both parts of this life are as truly connected as the root is to the stem, the tree with the fruit. He had first to affirm openly uncompromising dogmatism, and make it triumph in the Church, at the risk of embroiling himself, perhaps hopelessly, with public opinion before bringing to a diseased society the promises and consolations of a liberating Catholicism.

Already, at that time, the re-establishment of unity in Christianity was one of the questions of the day. The scandal of these divisions rightly occupied the thoughts of the disciples of that Master who said—"One flock, one Shepherd." A society was formed, in 1857, to work through prayer at the restoration of unity. Along with two hundred members of the English clergy were some Catholics, more zealous than enlightened. The Holy Office, consulted in 1864, had condemned the theory dear to the partisans of a sort of federation of the Churches, according to which there are three branches of Christianity—the Roman, the Eastern, and the English Churches. A protest was addressed to Cardinal Wiseman, even to the Holy Father. Manning was not unaware that this false ideal of Corporative Reunion, that is to say, the negotiation, as between equals, of a sort of treaty between the Churches, is often the chief obstacle to individual reunion, that is, the pure and simple submission to legitimate authority. In fact, in spite of the sophistry of the edifying formulas of the champions of this spurious federalism, there are only two conceptions possible ; that of the one visible, infallible Church, demanding submission,— the conception of Catholicism ;[1] and that of the invisible Church, never realizing its unity externally, but content with the mystical communion of souls —that is the Protestant conception.

Between the two, the hybrid notion of Anglicanism steps in, and borrowing from Protestantism its

---

[1] The Encyclical *Satis cognitum*, in reply to fresh attempts of Anglicanism to get itself recognized as a legitimate branch of the one universal Church, has just definitely laid down the Catholic principles in this matter.

173

refusal to recognize the divine right of the centre of unity, and taking from Catholicism its theory of the Church, endeavours to apply it to the most insular, the most local, the most dependent of Churches. Manning, who had made their trial, was pitiless to these claims. He declared that a single soul won over was worth more in his eyes than all these clergymen who were anxious to negotiate. The Pope, partly from Manning's prompting, wrote a reply which did not even grant (from fear of encouraging these illusions) the title of Reverend to these clergymen, and Manning set forth the Catholic doctrine in his Pastoral Letter of 1866. In it he affirmed that it was a question, not of re-establishing the unity of the Church,—there is only one Church, and the promises of Christ have guaranteed it the perfection of its unity as well as the unchangeableness of its faith,—but of bringing back to this Church, alone worthy of this name, all those who, by remaining separate from her, commit the sin of schism. This severity greatly displeased the Anglicans, especially Manning's former friends.

They did not comprehend this attitude with regard to a Church that Manning on his side regarded as all the more sinning, being nearer to the light, and seeing that her hypocritical pretences and fine externals kept more souls away from the light. Manning had come greatly to prefer the state of mind of the Dissenters, who were purely Protestants, to that of Anglo-Catholicism. He considered that the first sympathies of the Church should go "to those millions wandering here and there as sheep without a shepherd," to those classes that form "the heart of the English nation, to those souls for whom Christ died, and who have been robbed of their heritage by that Anglican schism," from which they have rightly separated themselves in their turn, and who, in "spite of the prejudices of education, often bring more sincerity, candour, and generosity into controversy" than the members of the English Church. There was a whole programme of action in these words, calculated to scandalize the Anglicans. Manning gave them another grievance in the attitude he took in the grave question of the Catholic youth going to the Oxford and Cambridge Universities.

The abolition of religious tests at the Universities, thus secularizing them in fact, seemed to authorize Catholic fathers of families in not depriving their children of the double privilege of high, intellectual education, and of a participation in that University life that is the best apprenticeship for life in the world. Newman had never ceased to feel a sort of home-sickness for those places where he had spent his happiest days, and where he had reigned as an absolute monarch. Since the failure of the project of founding a Catholic University at

Dublin, he lived retired at the Edgbaston Oratory, devoted to the direction of a secondary school. There had been some idea of placing him again at Oxford, at the head of a house of his community, to exercise a missionary activity on the scene of his former glory. He had even secured some land for that purpose; the project grew gradually; there was a dream of a Catholic College, affiliated to the University; Newman, quivering with very natural ardour, forgot that at Dublin, in 1851, he had forbidden Catholic youths to reside at Protestant Universities. The adversaries of co-education bestirred themselves. They obtained from Rome a condemnation of attendance at Protestant universities, and, still more severely, at unsectarian universities. Manning had worked hard to obtain this decree. Struck by the great inconveniences of Newman's plan, but unaware of the practical difficulties of such an enterprise, he already dreamt of the creation of that Catholic University that he was to found at Kensington under the direction of Monsignor Capel. This enterprise was eventually to cause him much anxiety, cost him much, morally and pecuniarily, and end in piteous failure. For the moment, this prohibition, in which Manning had so great a share, was keenly felt by Newman. From this time dates the permanent coolness of the relations between these two men, that famous disagreement, about which it is all the more necessary to speak clearly, as its story has been further misrepresented to Manning's detriment in Mr. Purcell's book.

For years before, the two great converts had been constantly opposed to each other. Under a superficial analogy was hidden an almost complete contrast of natures, temperaments, destinies. It was certain that over-zealous friends would remark with some bitterness upon the change that had taken place in the respective positions of Newman and Manning since their abjuration. Before it, Newman was the king of Oxford, the oracle of Anglo-Catholicism : Manning was only an adjutant, an ally in the field. After it, Newman lived in retirement, in a sort of disgrace, the head of a school for young boys; Manning was Archbishop of Westminster, Primate of England, the intimate confidant and trusted adviser of the Pope. Such a difference in their lives must, in itself alone, procure for the one all the favours, for the other all the severities of public opinion. Why should not the public have bestowed freely its marks of goodwill on the great intellect, the eminent writer, the honour of English literature, looked upon as having drawn upon himself the semi-disgrace in which he vegetated, by his courage in defending causes dear to the British nation ? Why should not the public have kept its severity for a man who seemed to consider it his task to defy it by espousing the most unpopular causes, and whose rapid advancement was attributed to the Vatican? Anglicans, Protestants, the Liberals themselves, willingly showed kindly feeling towards the great man whose incomparable services to the Church were rewarded by a sort of ostracism. They felt vaguely that Newman was still one of them, that he had never been this more than since his conversion; that English to the backbone, since he had come into direct contact with the realities of Catholicism, he had been cast back towards the half-solutions of a species of Anglican Gallicanism. On the other hand, they avenged themselves for Manning's uncompromising spirit, for his boldness in flinging down the challenge of his defence of the temporal power and infallibility, and of his aggressive and offensive Catholicism, by attributing these convictions to ambition and his success to intrigue. He was regarded then under this aspect. Disraeli himself, who sincerely admired him, and later knew him well, makes this a prominent feature in the rather brilliant and highly-coloured portrait that he gave of Manning in his novel of *Lothair*. His Cardinal Grandison is an improbable mixture of asceticism and Machiavelism. Friends naturally busied themselves in embittering the quarrel. Newman, willingly or unwillingly, was the centre of the opposition to all that went on at the Archbishop's residence. Perhaps Manning did not

sufficiently silence some imprudent remarks from
those about him. Opportunities of conflict were
not wanting—the reunion of Christendom, university
education, controversies relating to the temporal
power, to the *Syllabus*, and to infallibility. Nevertheless all these divergences would hardly have
signified much, had there not been incompatibility
of temperament also between the two. I have
already sketched these figures with their essential
differences : the student with his subtle thoughts,
past-master in the most skilful combats of minds,
sworn enemy of rash generalizations and ill-defined
assertions, in the main, sceptical by nature, like all
purely intellectual men; and the man of action,
ever on the breach, neither having nor taking the
time to polish his thoughts or to file his phrases,
going straight to his aim, the salvation of souls ;
loving to proceed by strong, plainly expressed
affirmations, hating deductions and arguments.
Newman was one of the renovators of apologetics,
a dialectician of high rank ; if he greatly opposed
and often humiliated reason, he also greatly loved
it and often appealed to it. Manning believed that
the priest's mission is to testify by his words, but
above all, by his life, to the supernatural truths of
revelation.

These wide, theoretical differences would not
have sufficed to embroil these two champions of
Catholicism, had not their natures been opposed.

If Manning was a man of authority, if he required from his subordinates the loyal obedience that he rendered to his superiors, Newman had ended by losing somewhat of the sense of reality in the artificial atmosphere in which he was confined. More than ever the idol of a circle, always surrounded by pupils believing his every word, and by followers ready to swear *in verba magistri;* slightly intoxicated—who would not have been so?—by the incense everywhere offered him even by Protestants and Liberals, Newman must have seen a certain aloofness, explicable only by personal interest, in the state of a mind radically opposed in everything to his, although both had followed the same path. This unjust view seemed to be confirmed by Manning's elevation. Between the Archbishop, advocate of papal infallibility, and the infallible Oratorian it was difficult to maintain satisfactory relations. The letters published by Mr. Purcell show, at least, that Manning was ever the first to seek for a reconciliation, the last to give up the hope of one. He begged Newman to come to his consecration; Newman consented, but in the most ungracious manner. When he was obliged to address any congratulations to the Archbishop, he contrived, with some of the art shown in saintly wars, to insert a sour epigram. When Manning one day at last wished by a frank, *vivâ voce* explanation to clear up these painful misunderstandings, he brought upon himself a refusal, and received from his former friend, whose hierarchical superior after all he was, an almost outrageous paper of accusations. In it Newman declared his incurable mistrust ; he accused Manning of constant contradiction between his words and conduct, and ended by saying emphatically, that each time he had had to do with the Archbishop of Westminster, he did not know whether he stood on his head or his heels. In thus forgetting charity and respect the author of this accusing document exposed himself to a cruel retort ; had not he himself been constantly accused of Jesuitism, of casuistry, and of duplicity, and had he not been obliged to reply by his *Apologia* to the attacks of Kingsley?[1] Manning did not reply quite in this tone, but he retorted on his correspondent with some of the latter's imputations. This unedifying correspondence continued for some time, with long explanations from Manning, and short, sharp replies from Newman. It ended the day when, following the

[1] The historian Froude said, one day about this time, to a friend who has recently published a volume of *Reminiscences*— "The other day I met Newman walking in the Park. Each movement of that man made me feel that one could not believe a single word of what he said " (A. K. H. B., *The Last Years of St. Andrews*, 1890—1895. London : 1896). This outburst from a man who had been not only the disciple but the friend of Newman, is more scandalous than unjust. Nevertheless it shows that there was a kind of reproach that Newman ought to have avoided using against his neighbour.

example of that prelate in the " Lutrin," who dismisses the canons *bewildered and blessed*, the illustrious Oratorian shot at his adversary this Parthian shaft—" Meanwhile I intend to say seven masses for your benefit, in the midst of the difficulties and anxieties of your ecclesiastical duties."

Manning, although surprised, replied *tit for tat*—"I am much obliged to you for your kind intention of saying seven masses for my benefit, and I shall have great pleasure in celebrating one for your benefit, each month during the coming year."

This clerical bickering was happily not quite the last word between two men of this kind. After the accession of Leo XIII., the prolonged injustice of the Court of Rome towards the great athlete of the intellectual restoration of Catholicism was repaired. The Archbishop of Westminster was not the last of those who demanded the red hat for the Edgbaston recluse. Unhappily, a regrettable misunderstanding nearly changed this natural opportunity for reconciliation into a fresh cause of dispute; Manning was too hasty in believing that the scruples of a man who rather liked to be entreated, and to name his own conditions, were to be taken as a definite refusal; Newman committed a more serious fault in attributing double dealing to the Archbishop, from an error of the latter, arising from the difficulty of understanding the expressions of his subtle casuistry. In the end, all was explained.

Later, the two Cardinals met twice in London. It is characteristic of these two men, that while Manning opened his arms to embrace the adversary who had dealt him such sharp strokes with so keen-edged a rapier, Newman, on his return to the Oratory at Edgbaston, expressed only astonishment at this fraternal embrace.

Meanwhile, the Archbishop of Westminster found himself called to play a part of the first order on the stage of important affairs. The Definition of the dogma of the personal infallibility of the Sovereign Pontiff was one of the questions of the day. This story is still so recent that it is difficult to write it with suitable impartiality. Up till now, the public at large has perhaps regarded it too much from the accounts given by opponents. The Opposition was chiefly recruited from the camp of that Liberal Catholicism whose noble champions, Montalembert, Gratry, Dupanloup, Lacordaire, have so rightly won the sympathies of all generous minds. Doubtless, in France, almost all those who had opposed the Definition, submitted as docile children of the Church. They had the less trouble in doing this, as they were only fulfilling their rudimentary duty as Catholics, and as most of them had questioned only the expediency of this decision. At the same time many still feel a sort of prejudice against the chief promoters of the Council's decree. Two considerations seem, however, likely to remove this impression. First of all, the ulterior development of the destiny of Old Catholicism, that is to say, of that fraction of the opponents, especially in Germany, who did not bow down before the proclamation of the doctrine, is scarcely calculated to awaken very keen sympathy. If ever a Church or sect rested with all its weight upon the civil power, if ever a new schism believed it could profit, not only from the favours of the State, but also by a persecution of the rival Church, such as the *Kulturkampf*, Old Catholicism in Germany did this. There are, no doubt, among the clergy and the lay members of this little flock, men worthy of all respect; the name of Döllinger was in itself a tower of strength. Nevertheless, it cannot be concealed that this pretended reform came to nought —moreover, that it deserved to do so—like all so-called spiritual movements that appeal to the secular arm, and offer in exchange for its protection the services of a State religion. On the other hand, the Definition of the dogma of Infallibility has not produced the results predicted by its adversaries. It has, on the contrary, seemed to a large section of thinkers that this consummation of the work of concentrating the spiritual authority in the hands of the Vicar of Jesus Christ had in it something providential. On the eve of events that were to strip the Holy See of its patrimony, and reduce the Papacy to the position of a purely ideal power, it was not a trifling matter, that around the brow of a Pontiff, reduced to the state of an old, feeble priest, there should shine the aureole of a divine prerogative. And since then, has not this power, so carefully guaranteed and limited by the Constitution *De romano pontifice*, served especially for the realization of that generous dream, formed by the Liberal Catholics, that is to say, the adversaries of the dogma ? Does not the pontificate of Leo XIII., thanks to this great work of the reign of Pius IX., prepare the fulfilment of the ideal, too early formed and too imperiously pursued by Lamennais and the editors of the *Avenir* ? A Papacy raised sufficiently above the region of self-interest, passions, and selfish rivalry to take the lofty direction of the movement of social reform, without ceasing to be the keystone of human society ;—a Church firmly seated on the rock of unity, and sure enough of its divine mandate to offer to a suffering generation the remedy for all its woes—was not this the object, eagerly sought for by all those Catholics, smitten by a desire for the reconciliation of Christianity with the age ? Whatever may be thought of the realization of this dream, the man who clearly conceived the idea of the close connection of the two parts of this programme, the man who wished the Papacy to be mistress of the Church and the

Church to be the servant of humanity, deserves indeed that men should free themselves from party spirit and its prejudices, to appreciate his work fairly.

Before, during, and after the Council, Manning was one of the most ardent champions of the Definition. He loved to recall the nickname of Diabolus Concilii bestowed on him by his adversaries. At St. Peter's Jubilee, in 1868, he was in Rome with five hundred and twenty of his colleagues. He and the Bishop of Ratisbon vowed to procure the proclamation of the dogma of infallibility, and to say daily special prayers to that effect. Although the Bull of Convocation of September 13, 1868, did not expressly state the question, the Archbishop of Westminster hastened, none the less, to present two petitions to the Pope in favour of the Definition, which came from his diocese and from the Oratory at Brompton. During fourteen months, Europe was stirred by the preparation for one of those assemblies that had not been seen in Christendom for three centuries, since the end of the Council of Trent. The Press was full of violent polemics, mostly indulged in by the *Augsburg Gazette*, the *Civiltà Cattolica*, and the *Univers*, and in which the Bishop of Orleans, Monsignor Dupanloup, took a vigorous part. Four great Commissions of cardinals and prelates, respectively presided over by their Eminences Bilio, Caterini, de Reisach, and Bizzari, drew up in full details the *schemata* relative to the dogma, to the canon law, to the mixed politico-religious questions, and to the Regulars. The choice of the theological counsellors who were to help the Fathers of the Council was an important business. Dupanloup wished, but in vain, to have Newman for his counsellor. The English bishops had passed him over, whether from believing in an improbable report that the Pope wished to have direct aid from his views on this matter, or from his being regarded with disfavour at Rome through his opposition to the dogma of Infallibility. The struggle proved singularly sharp and obstinate, its issue being for a time doubtful. Döllinger was not content with employing the legitimate weapons of theology and erudition, nor even with denouncing the triumph of the Jesuits, while reproaching Manning for having a convert's zeal. He did not scruple to appeal to the civil power, and to claim the revival of the *veto* of crowned heads in the name of a would-be Liberalism, and in the interest of the principles of modern society. In the address adopted by the German bishops at Fulda, they took the narrower ground of the inopportuneness of the Definition. The threat of intervention by that Liberal Catholic party which had just obtained power in France with the

Ollivier-Daru Ministry, was thought to lurk behind
the learned, heavy dissertations of Monsignor
Maret's great work. Monsignor Dupanloup was
untiring in his eloquent protests. Manning had
issued a Pastoral Letter on the burning subject.
The Bishop of Orleans plainly accused him of
heresy, and this fiery controversialist, who did not
understand English, had to be informed that he
had condemned a mistake of the French translator.

The time for the Council drew near, and
Manning set out. At Paris he saw M. Thiers,
who uttered the most edifying deistical sentiments,
and said naïvely, "Do not make life too hard for
us! Do not condemn the principles of '89!" M.
Guizot declared that "the temporal power was the
last pillar of European order," and that he saw in
the Council "the only moral power that may restore
peace to the world." The first business of this
assembly was to elect deputations or commissions
in which the Episcopate of each nationality had
one or several representatives. The choice of the
English bishops fell, not on Manning, but on
Grant. The Italians made up for this by electing
the Archbishop of Westminster. It does not enter
into my plan to give in detail the history of the
Vatican Council; I must be content to describe the
part taken in it by Manning. This part was three-
fold; in the Council, amongst his colleagues, in

preparatory work and general discussions; outside it, with the Pope and with the distinguished agent sent by England, without accrediting him at Rome. His activity was immense. It equalled that of his great adversary, Monsignor Dupanloup, who, to Manning's astonishment, sent off bales of written papers daily. It was a matter of conscience with both; if the one declared that he "shed tears of blood at the thought of all the souls that would be lost through an inopportune definition," the other sincerely believed that the salvation of the Church and the world depended on the promulgation of this truth. Inside the Council Manning struggled energetically, first, to get the *postulatum*, or proposal to place the question on the orders of the day, signed and presented; then to obtain a favourable report from the delegation *de postulatis*, or initiatory commission; afterwards to put aside the demands for adjournment or amendments, and to secure voting on the main point. Here he displayed all the qualities that would have made him a Member of Parliament of the highest order. At the same time, according to good judges, he showed himself the prince of diplomatists. The familiar intercourse granted him by the fatherly goodness of Pius IX. secured him valuable advantages, which he did not hesitate to make use of. He had the *entrée* of a private staircase and door in the Pope's apartments at the Vatican, and he has described the astonishment of the diplomatists or ecclesiastics who patiently waited for their turn of audience in the ante-rooms of the Sovereign Pontiff, at seeing the exit of this visitor whom they had not seen enter. He used this privilege several times, in order to give energetic counsels to the Pope, or to stir him up to decisive resolutions; never did he employ it more usefully than the day when, having learnt that Döllinger, being, through the Opposition, in possession of the *schema*, was preparing to urge the Bavarian Government to initiate a preliminary intervention of the Powers, he hastened to ask the Holy Father to relieve him of his oath of secrecy, that he might communicate the true state of affairs to Mr. Odo Russell, and enable him to prevent a vexatious decision of the Gladstone Cabinet.

It was especially in his relations with Mr. Odo Russell that Manning gave proof of the qualities that would have made him an eminent ambassador or statesman. He had become intimate with this high-born diplomatist, who for ten years had filled with distinction an unofficial mission at Rome. Whig and Protestant though he was, the nephew of Lord John Russell had conceived a passionate liking for the Eternal City, wished to remain there, and had become a convinced partisan of the continuance of the temporal power and of the Definition of the dogma of Infallibility. Such a state of mind in her Majesty's representative made him a valuable acquaintance.

Besides the weekly interviews and conversations, the Archbishop and the diplomatist met each Saturday (the Council not sitting that day) for a long walk in the country. The talk turned upon everything, from the great, eternal problems to the trifles that constituted the food of those whom Louis Veuillot called the gossips of the Council. Manning then told his companion, and through him Gladstone and Lord Clarendon, all that he could and ought to tell them. It was a successful stroke, thus to obtain a docile and safe instrument in the diplomatist, who at Berlin later was to play a hard-fought, closely-contested game with Bismarck The fierce activity of the Opposition was doomed to be unsuccessful, from the moment when the Governments on whom it had relied decided on non - interference. In the English Cabinet, it needed all the influence of Mr. Odo Russell, with his chief, Lord Clarendon, to counterbalance in the mind of Mr. Gladstone the weighty advice of Sir John Acton.[1] He was the friend of Döllinger, and the great leader of the Press campaign in England and Germany, who energetically supported the Munich Cabinet's proposal of inter-

[1] Now Lord Acton, formerly in the Gladstone-Rosebery Ministry from 1892 to 1893, and appointed to the Chair of Modern History at Cambridge as successor to Sir John Seeley.

vention. France, tempted at first to make Napoleon III. play the part of heir to Louis XIV., by reviving the *veto* of the Crown, was absorbed in the grave preoccupations of the plébiscite and foreign policy. In vain the minority in the Council resisted, keeping up outside a threatening agitation, employing obstruction inside; they exhausted every means of adjournment, made a display of the probable number of their votes, which they estimated at one hundred and forty or one hundred and fifty, by adding to the *non placet* the *juxta modum;* lastly, they tried to intimidate the majority by glorifying the moral force of an opposition containing more than half the bishops of France and Germany. This rather self-satisfied superiority met with some opposition in the debates. Cardinal Bilio considered the speech made by the Archbishop of Westminster in the general discussion as worthy to rank with the harangues of Strossmayer and Dupanloup. Manning himself shrewdly said—"They were wise, we were fools. Well, strange to say, it happened that the wise were always wrong and the fools always right."

Events hurried on. Deceived in the hope of intervention by the civil power, and beaten on their proposal to prorogue the Council *sine die*, the opposing bishops either left Rome or decided to abstain from voting. On May 14, 1870, the general discussion was opened on the *schema de*

Romano Pontifice. On July 13, by a majority of
four hundred and fifty-one votes against eighty-
eight *non placet* and sixty-two *placet juxta modum*,
the chapter on the Pontifical Infallibility and the
immediate jurisdiction of the Holy See was adopted
in general Congregation. The Pope, petitioned
by a delegation from the minority to interfere in
favour of conciliation, did not think fit to do so.
Five days later, the Council held its fourth sitting,
and ratified its previous vote by five hundred and
thirty-three *placet* against two *non placet.*

The next day, July 19, war was declared between
France and Germany. In the whirlwind of these
tragic events, purely religious questions were
banished to the background. It might have seemed
as though Providence had allowed the Papacy to
reach the final stage of a slow development,
only to hurl it down a deeper abyss; *ut lapsu
graviore ruat.* The Italian troops, meekly following the heels of the victorious Prussians, entered
Rome, September 20, by the inglorious breach of
the *Porta Pia.* Was this the end of the spiritual
authority as well as of the temporal power of the
Holy See? Was this the chastisement for the
proclamation of Infallibility? Manning believed
not. While declaring that law had been violated
in this sacrilegious usurpation of the patrimony of
St. Peter, he saw fully that a new era was opening
for the Papacy, when, deprived of its temporal

possessions, reduced to its sole spiritual prerogative, it would become the arbiter of nations and of
kings, could it only employ rightly its royal
poverty and its ideal power. In his eyes, the
Definition of the dogma of Infallibility on the eve
of this brutal invasion was, to the highest degree,
providential. Perhaps, in the latter years of his
life, when his ideas had ripened, and his hatred of
incompatible alliances between the things of God
and His Church and temporal things had been
firmly knit, he would have avowed, without much
hesitation, that there was something providential
in this destruction of the temporal power. Not
that he dreamt of dishonourable and impossible
compromises between the Vatican and the Quirinal,
or that he wavered in the imprescriptible claim for
sovereignty due to the Head of the Catholic
Church. The Archbishop of Westminster was
no partisan of those spurious Concordats that
would reduce the Father of the Faithful to the
position of a chaplain to the House of Savoy,—
converted as Manning was, through the manly
practice of the *régime* of a poor and independent
Church entirely separated from the State, to the
doctrine of pure and simple liberty, as shown
in England and America. A devoted son, a
faithful friend of that Pius IX. who rewarded
him by raising him to the Cardinalship in 1875,
from whom he had the consolation of receiving

a tender farewell, "*Addio, Carissimo*," on his death-bed, Manning would have believed himself a traitor to his benefactor and to his own past, by lending himself to the crooked diplomacy of those conciliators who were ready to sacrifice all the rights of conscience for a smile from the great ones of this world.

He has shown in his private diary that he equally repudiated the two schools which aim at the spiritual quite as much as at the temporal abdication of the Pope; one, by pretending to count upon a miracle, the other, by preaching inaction as the most sacred duty. In 1876 he wrote—" We must know whether we ought to shut ourselves up in an ark, like Noah, or whether we ought not rather, like all the Pontiffs since Leo the Great, to act upon the world." He added—" The parable of the lost sheep should settle the question." Thus again, the source of Manning's policy, the secret of the development which, later, was to transform the champion of the temporal power and of Infallibility into the apostle of a reforming Papacy and of social Catholicism, were to be found in the depths of a truly priestly conscience, and in the eager desire to save souls.

This noble conception of the Papacy freeing itself by freeing the Church, conquering the world by dint of serving it, was the inspiration of the last twenty years of his life. It naturally led him at times to leave the purely ecclesiastical ground, yet

he still fought tough battles there. The most
redoubtable adversary with whom he had to cross
swords was Mr. Gladstone, who profited by his
retirement into private life in 1874 to maintain
in his "Vaticanismes," and other pamphlets, the
impossibility for Catholics to preserve loyal allegiance to their Sovereign, if they accepted the dogma
of Infallibility. It cost Manning much to throw
himself into the controversy, which again interrupted
for fifteen years a friendship previously broken off
by his conversion, and only gradually renewed since
1865. But, as usual, he did not shirk this painful
duty. He showed the same youthful zeal in this
matter as he did in the administration of his diocese
and in the exercise of his spiritual functions, in
preaching, in the direction of souls, and in the education of the clergy, so dear to his heart. His less
frequent journeys to Rome must be ascribed to his
increasing years. Created a Cardinal in 1875, he
wore the purple with a simple dignity that increased
its splendour. Ascetic in his habits, he followed
the most frugal regimen, drinking only water; [1] but

[1] The Cardinal, formerly a Temperance man, became a
total abstainer. One day, at a Temperance meeting, he said
—"I drink wine only at my doctor's orders"; a voice cried,
"Change him." He did so. Another time, he was urging
an Irish workman, whom he had met in the street, to take the
pledge, adding, by way of argument, "I have taken it." Although Manning had not said who he was, the man recognized
him, and, humorous like all his countrymen, he remarked
with a wink of the eye—"Ah! sir, I expect you needed it."

he kept a hospitable table for his friends, simple but suitable to his position. In England, the hostilities he had encountered at the beginning were not quite at an end; more than one cause for hatred still smouldered, but the enemy's voice was silenced and his authority amongst Catholics almost equalled his popularity outside their Church. He was still powerful at Rome, although he was grieved to notice there a certain decadence and narrowing of spirit.

His power at Rome was felt, not only under Pius IX., but after the death of that Pontiff, at the Conclave, when a group of Italian Cardinals, amongst whom were their Eminences Franchi, Bilio, Bartolini, Monaco, and Nina, offered him the tiara in all sincerity. He was one of the chief promoters and causes at the Conclave of the election of Cardinal Pecci. This fact disposes of the story of the antagonism between Leo XIII. and Manning. If there did not exist the same intimate friendship between them as there had been between Pius IX. and Manning, the new Pope carefully lavished on the Cardinal Archbishop of Westminster, during the journey this prelate made *ad limina apostolorum*, every mark of well-merited confidence and deference, and followed his advice about persons and things in England. To refute such foolish stories, we need only remember the share that Manning took in the triumph of Cardinal

Gibbons' theories when these were laid before the Court of Rome, and also point out the complete harmony of the great Encyclicals of Leo XIII. with all the religious and social plans of the Archbishop of Westminster.

III

SINCE the Vatican Council had realized Manning's ecclesiastical programme, he could carry out his social plans without fear of being attacked in the rear, or of seeing the ground sink under his feet. He had been naturally led to these plans by the charity that had brought him into contact with all the sufferings of our time. In the frightful dens of the East End of London he had learnt to know that poverty, of which material want and destitution are only some of the features, and not the worst; that poverty which is degraded by the conditions of its existence, which is prevented by the very excess of its needs from rising again to the surface, and which is made criminal in spite of itself by the infamy of its circumstances. He had gone down to the depths of that hell, compared with which the hell of Dante is an abode of the blessed. There he had come across that hero of Protestant charity, Lord Shaftesbury. One feels the purest, the highest satisfaction in seeing these two great Christians, placed at the antipodes of thought and life, one the Cardinal Archbishop of the Holy Roman Church, an Ultramontane, the other, an inflexible Protestant, full of Biblical indignation against "the great whore of Babylon,"—to see these two grasp hands and consult each other in the name of that charity into which mere love of humanity has developed through the religion of Christ. Both Conservatives by birth, position, instinct, and habit of mind, they acquired, from contact with these realities, a socialism *sui generis*, against which the demonstrations of political economy were powerless. We are all familiar with the part played by Lord Shaftesbury in protective legislation for childhood and labour. I have now to describe Manning's activity on the same lines.

His habit of mind, aided by circumstances, had, after his abjuration, for long kept him apart from unsectarian Associations. In 1871, he was asked to join the Mansion House Committee for sending aid to Paris after the siege. This was his beginning. Since then, there was hardly a philanthropic or moral work, outside the battle-ground of the rival Churches, in which the Archbishop of Westminster did not take a share. It was an instructive and curious spectacle to see the welcome and position granted to this prince of the Roman Church, in a purely Protestant country, where the law, quite recently, had recognized a Catholic priest only through his civil and political disabilities. Personally, Manning cared little for this homage; he valued it only as a precedent to fix the position of his successor, or raise the condition of his colleagues. He carried this feeling of solidarity to such an extent that, later, when the last barriers were removed and he was invited to Court or to Marlborough House, he accepted these favours of the Queen, or of the heir to the throne, only so far as they were paid, not to himself personally, but to his rank, and as a benefit to his Episcopal brethren. Another very important innovation was the summoning this Cardinal Archbishop to join those Royal Commissions which English Governments create, to inquire about matters of public interest. Manning sat with the Prince of Wales upon the Commission for Workmen's Dwellings, taking a very important part. The Ministers also applied to him for information about Temperance legislation. He did not think himself free to avoid these additional labours, first and chiefly on account of their intrinsic usefulness, then also with a view to the manifest triumph of the principles of toleration, which would be secured by his presence on these official bodies. Nevertheless, his heart was not so deeply engaged in these works of administration as in his own works for raising and helping the poor.

It cannot be too often repeated that it was through the royal road of charity, through observing the

fundamental precept of the Gospel, in walking as
closely as possible in the footsteps of Jesus Christ,
that Manning attained to that wide, bold view of
our social evils, and the best way of remedying
them; it is a reply to certain *doctrinaire* assertions
that theoretic devotion to social reform would
always be in inverse proportion to practical activity
for the relief of poverty. The first work to which
he devoted himself was that of Temperance. He
had seen, with his own eyes, the dire effects of
alcohol, perhaps the greatest scourge of our civilization; families destroyed, children, the innocent heirs
to every bodily and moral defect, victims of ill-
treatment or desertion; drunkards, slaves of a
pitiless tyrant, slowly ruined in health, loathing
work, forgetful of the road to the workshop and to
the Church; in short, a hell upon earth, in the
centre of our great towns. Before such a state of
things, Manning was not one to stand with folded
arms. He appealed not only to every resource of
religion—though in this holy crusade this was ever
the best of his forces—but he had recourse to every
means of action, to combination, enthusiasm, all
that awakens and strengthens the conscience, all
that moves and affects the popular mind. He
founded and propagated the League of the Cross.
He wore his Cardinal's robe when on the platforms
of public meetings. For a long time he met only
with repugnance and hostility from the clergy and

pious laity. His resolutely modern and popular methods frightened the prudent and reasonable, repelled the fastidious. He was reproached with borrowing some of his noisy means of propaganda from that Salvation Army for which, within the limits set down by his impeccable orthodoxy, he openly expressed warm sympathy. He was blamed for being on too familiar terms with his Leaguers, especially with those tried helpers whom he had formed into his body-guard. The affectedly grave and starched Pharisees whose horizon has never extended beyond the walls of a sacristy were disturbed and shocked by his annual fête of the League of the Cross at the Crystal Palace, with its quasi-military organization, its banners, bands, distinctive ribbons, its review before the Commander-in-chief, the Prince of the Church, who harangued the crowd to the accompaniment of wild applause. More than this, some grave doctors expressed doubts as to the perfect doctrinal correctness of a movement appearing to give to temperance, to abstinence even, a disproportionate place amongst the theological virtues.

Manning let them talk. *Si hominibus placerem non essem servus Dei:* that was all his reply to his critics. He went his way, devoting to this propaganda every moment of liberty, and even his short summer holidays during several years ; himself practising abstinence, and being accessible at any moment to his staff, or to any repentant drunkard who came to ask help and advice. Such zeal must have its reward. By degrees, as the work grew, objections vanished. Hundreds of the secular priests, and the religious orders as a whole, took part in this activity. Branches of the League of the Cross spread all over the country, and reckoned its members by tens of thousands. The Cardinal's body-guard rose to 1400; children joined in great numbers. Manning could truly write when face to face with death—"One of my greatest joys is having saved many poor drunkards."

We must now turn to the second branch of this activity, that which concerned children. They always had the first claim upon him. His first impulse when he was made Archbishop was to think joyfully of all he could do for the poor children, unhelped by the Church, and whose numbers he estimated at twenty thousand in his diocese alone. It is well known how Manning, after having purchased a large plot of ground, turned all his efforts and the donors' gifts to the education of childhood,[1] much to the indignation of those

---

[1] Manning allowed the poor children of the neighbourhood to use as a playground the enclosed land intended for the site of the future Cathedral. As for "the Archbishop's house," which he bought and which is the residence of his successor, it was an immense, bare building, formerly a club for the non-commissioned officers in the Guards. He was attracted by the size and austere simplicity of the building, where he lived till the end.

Christians who prefer a monument of hewn stone to an edifice of living souls, and who could not forgive him for not considering himself bound to complete the erection of the Cathedral planned and begun by Wiseman. It was the time when England, during the Gladstone Ministry and under Mr. Forster's direction, adopted that great system of popular education that gave such a powerful impulse to the diffusion of knowledge, but which put forward, in an urgent and pointed form, the question of religious teaching. Public opinion had not yet grasped the great truth that liberty of conscience and parental rights are as much injured by public education, given in the name of the State and at the expense of ratepayers, but from which the names of God and religion are banished, as by a system of sectarian education imposed on every one. It was therefore necessary to keep up and even develop Church schools, especially for a minority, such as the Catholics; it was further necessary to open and support, at great cost, orphanages, industrial schools, reformatories for thousands of children who would have risked losing their faith in non-Catholic establishments. This was Manning's work, and it was colossal. The proof of his success is first, those large, handsome diocesan and parochial schools;[1] next, the important part played by the

[1] In 1891 there were 3204 Catholic children in the London orphanages and voluntary schools, all being periodically

Archbishop of Westminster on the Royal Commission for Elementary Education, where he was truly the inspirer of the recommendations of the Report in favour of amendment of the Act of 1870. It is, in fact, the Bill which was brought before the House of Commons, then withdrawn with a promise of being again brought forward next year, and which Cardinal Vaughan and his suffragans recognize, in spite of many omissions, as a sincere effort to satisfy the demands of the Church.

Manning, however, did not restrict himself to this somewhat professional form of activity. The man who said that "the undried tears of a child cried to God as loudly as blood spilt on the ground," was the born patron of every work for the protection and defence of childhood. He especially collaborated most zealously with the great unsectarian society founded and directed by a Nonconformist minister, the Rev. Benjamin Waugh, for the prevention of cruelty to children. When the editor of the *Pall Mall Gazette* began his campaign against criminal sensuality and its outrages on minors, Mr. Stead had no more intrepid ally than the Cardinal Archbishop, who even carried his generosity to the length of refraining from publicly disavowing the indiscretions into

visited by a Diocesan Inspector; 2253 children were in charity asylums, and 22,580 other children in the Free Catholic Schools of the diocese.

which zeal led his *protégé*. Some of those about Manning were much scandalized at this fashion of committing himself with any one who seemed moved by a truly generous spirit to serve humanity. Those who fancied they could instruct him upon the danger of these acquaintances, did not attempt it again; the priest, the prelate, the prince, rose and showed them their right place.

All this activity could not fail to bear fruit in such a mind as Manning's, open till the last to the teachings of experience. In politics, he had begun as a pure Conservative, a Tory of the strictest order. So long as he was an Anglican, he remained faithful to that party. He viewed every question in its connection with the National Church. Christianity and its inspirations were somewhat stifled by ecclesiasticism. After his conversion, all this changed. He was no longer a member of the Church of England, but of the Church in England. The civil power was no longer for him the natural protector as well as the regulator of spiritual power. His logical mind was not long in modifying greatly his conclusions on all these points. He called himself a Mosaic Radical, a disciple of Moses, to show the fundamental conservatism of his advanced opinions and their Biblical origin. This is not the first time that the Old Testament has been responsible for a transformation of this kind; did not Voltaire say irreverently of a prophet whose frankness of speech could hardly be equalled by the socialists of to-day—"That fellow Amos was capable of anything."

Amongst the new feelings that Manning drew from his change of religion, we must place in the first rank his love for Ireland. He began by venerating in her the Island of Saints and the Land of Martyrs, watered with the blood that England, associating the spirit of persecution with the spirit of domination, had shed there in torrents. Although he had denounced Fenianism as sinful, in common with all secret societies, his daily and familiar relations with a race that formed the large majority of his flock soon inspired him with that enthusiastic and compassionate affection which the Irish never fail to call forth in those who know them. He was the earliest amongst the English to accept the idea of Home Rule as the only possible solution of a problem that may prove insoluble. When Gladstone in 1886 adopted a policy that he had faithfully opposed so long as he could believe in the success of the only alternative acceptable to a Liberal, namely, the carrying out of a programme of organic reforms, Manning drew near to his old friend, with whom he had been on distant terms since their controversy on the Vatican decrees. The Irish in the large towns adored him. On St. Patrick's Day, which he had converted into St. Patrick's Truce, with the hope of rescuing some victims of alcohol, the Archbishop's name was always cheered. When he celebrated the twenty-fifth anniversary of his Episcopate, all the Nationalist members of Parliament, Protestants and Catholics, with the heretic Parnell at their head, offered their congratulations at his residence. This grieved all those Catholics, numerous in England as elsewhere, who cannot distinguish the cause of God and of the Church from that of social order, political conservatism, and "légitimité." In his last years, Manning scandalized them so often that once more hardly mattered. People would have gladly attributed these freaks of the Cardinal to the score of age and of the isolation with which he more and more surrounded himself; but his vigorous appearance when he said Mass, the brightness of his eagle-glance, the majesty of his bearing, the inspiring animation of his mind, contradicted these ideas. The Cardinal was keeping a much more disagreeable surprise in store for his detractors. During the last years of his life, he was to preach in words and actions that doctrine of Catholic socialism, or rather of social Catholicism, which is indeed the most hateful of new doctrines to those faithful who look upon the Church as the guardian of their interests, and upon religion as the best safeguard of property.

I should not call the doctrine *new*, for it was Manning's special desire to restore old Catholic doctrine on these essential points, and to borrow from St. Thomas Aquinas, whose wisdom, enlightened by revelation, is as full upon this head as upon others, the fruitful principles of a social science unspoiled by materialism in its premisses, or by partiality in its deductions. I can only sketch very slightly the numerous and remarkable works which the Cardinal produced on this subject, either as articles in the chief Reviews, or as polemical letters in the columns of the *Times*, or even as Pastoral Letters. His theory rested upon a few very simple, general ideas. Political economy was to him a moral science, and the conclusions of the abstract study of riches were valuable only so far as they were subordinated to the universal laws of conscience. He considered that labour, relegated too long into the second rank, and deprived of the protection which is so greatly needed, should be treated on the same footing as capital. Man was the sole economic unit, the essential social quantity; the human being with his physical and moral needs, his aspirations, his rights. The aim of society should be, not the production of riches, but the production of the greatest possible happiness of the greatest number under the rule of the moral law. No social axiom was in his eyes more chimerical than that advocating the false dogma of *laissez faire*, or of the non-intervention of the State. The whole economic history of humanity had been the violation of this so-called principle, especially for the profit of capitalists. Of late, the protective legislation for labour with which Lord Shaftesbury was connected, had begun to restore the equilibrium. Manning thought it the more deplorable that this should be arrested under pretext of respecting the fictions of a certain kind of political economy. There was still a vast amount to be accomplished, and justice, no less than the safety of society, was concerned in the continuation of the enterprise.

Since the year 1873 Manning had been inspired by these ideas, though at that time German State Socialism had scarcely begun, to assist Joseph Arch in his formation of Rural Trades Unions. A lecture which Manning delivered on the rights and dignity of labour set forth his principles. In it he sketched that social organization which was ever in his thoughts, and which in many respects resembled the old system of guilds. While repudiating any revolutionary sympathies, he plainly decided in favour of legalized hours of daily work, and after having shown some of the effects of unlimited competition and un-restrained action of Supply and Demand, he con-cluded with these words—" These things cannot—they must not last. The amassing of riches, huge

in the over-charged electrical atmosphere of London, the strike might turn to civil war. Happily the dockers were led by sensible men—Burns, Mann, Tillett—whom they obeyed with admirable discipline. Only sixteen days after the beginning of the struggle, the Cardinal was asked to take part in efforts towards conciliation. In an interview with the Directors, he begged them to yield on the question of wages, alike in view of their own interests—that is, to avert an imminent revolution— and in pity for the sufferings of the poor. A committee, under the presidency of the Lord Mayor, was formed, and included the Cardinal, the Bishop of London, who before long, relinquished responsibilities too heavy for him, Mr. Sidney Buxton, and some others. On Manning and Buxton fell all the weight of the negotiations. Convinced of the justice of the chief claims of the strikers, they worked with rare energy to obtain large concessions from the Directors. A compromise was suggested: the labourers were to have the rate of wages they demanded, the famous "tanner," or 6d. per hour, but the new tariff was not to come into force until March 1, 1890, viz. after a delay of six months. Burns and Tillett declared that it would be impossible to induce their fellow workers to accept this delay; Manning did his best with the Directors to have the date altered to January 1. This was the extreme limit of their concessions.

The compromise had to be sanctioned by the strikers, already accusing their leaders of treason. The Cardinal and Mr. Buxton went to the dockers' head-quarters in the crowded district of Poplar. A stormy meeting was held in the school-room of the Catholic church in Kirby Street. The dockers for the first time experienced the results of union. They thought themselves sure of victory. To ask them to wait for three months before they received in full the cash-result of these weeks of privations and sacrifices was to make an appeal to reason against instinct in creatures of instinct only. The Cardinal, convinced as he was of the justice of their cause, knew that this was the only means of securing their triumph, and that the Directors needed only a pretext in order to withdraw their concessions. For nearly five hours—from 5 to 10 p.m.—this old man of eighty-three, this Prince of the Church, pleaded with friendly and passionate eloquence the interests of the labourers and their families. He drew tears from the driest eyes in making an eloquent appeal to their love for wives and children. His cause was gained. These simple, rough men were intensely moved. One believed he saw the statue of the Madonna standing behind the venerable orator's head, give a sign of approval. The true miracle, however, was the conquest of those simple-minded and rough natures

by the old priest who never served Christ better
than when he secured this peace.

We must part from Manning with this final
scene. Only a few months of life remained to
him ; the shades of evening fell more and more
closely upon him. His health was too feeble to
allow him to leave his residence to go to the
Athenæum Club, where he greatly delighted in the
refreshing society of Ruskin, Bryce, Gladstone, or
even of some English bishop. He felt isolated,
even though surrounded by the love of a whole
people and the veneration of his Church. His
thoughts voluntarily retraced the past. He gave
himself up to a lengthy self-examination, reviewed
the course of his long life, and rendered thanks to
God for having revealed to him "the fulness of His
grace." He humiliated himself for his errors and
faults, and when he felt discouraged by comparing
his career with that of Shaftesbury, of Gladstone,
or even of Macaulay, he enumerated the five great
truths to which he had testified, viz. the Unity of
the Church, the Rule of Divine Faith, the Infallibility of the Church and of its Head, the office of
the Holy Spirit, the temporal power of the Vicar
of Jesus Christ. He added to these, the three great
causes to which he had devoted himself: the religious education of children, Temperance, and the
education of the clergy. A weariness of life came

upon him, but he never felt the fear of death. "There are people," he said, "who are afraid to speak of their end. As for me, I like to do so, it is a help in self-preparation, and it removes all sadness and terror. It is a good thing to fill one's thoughts with the light and beauty of the world beyond the tomb. That is what inspired St. Paul in his desire to depart." This simple, radiant faith was truly most fitting to soothe this great Christian's death-bed.

For more than two years he felt calmly his feebleness increase. At the beginning of the year 1892 he understood that his last hours were approaching; after six days' illness, on January 13, he received the last sacraments, and made his solemn profession of faith before the Chapter of Westminster. During his last night three friends watched over him, Monsignor Vaughan, his successor, Canon Johnson, his secretary, and Dr. Gasquet, his physician. At daybreak on the 14th, while Monsignor Vaughan was saying Mass for him in his oratory, the soul of Henry Edward Manning, Cardinal Archbishop of Westminster, was called back to God.

Almost at the same time died a young prince in the direct line of succession to the English crown, the Duke of Clarence. This national mourning in no way interfered with the immense outburst of sorrow which the news of the Cardinal's death caused. The working, populous districts of London

felt like orphans. Amongst the crowds which filed
in close ranks through the mortuary chapel where
lay the remains of the Archbishop, dressed in the
Cardinal's scarlet robes, were, with his fellow
bishops, members of his clergy, laymen of his flock,
neophytes whom he had brought to the Church,
his penitents, his friends whom he had always
received with his habitual graciousness, and people
of the most varied opinions and diverse origin, who
had enjoyed his generous and tolerant hospitality;
and with all these passed a nameless crowd, some
decently clad, others wan and ragged, who had
come to look for the last time at the emaciated
features of the friend of the poor, the Cardinal of
the people. His funeral took place January 21,
at the Brompton Oratory. In that vast sanctuary,
assembled there to pay him the last marks of
respect, were representatives of the Church, the
aristocracy, politics, and the governing class; but
the most imposing manifestation of grief was outside. The streets were filled with immense masses
of people. The League of the Cross with its
banners, the Irish National League, the United
Kingdom Alliance, the London Trades Unions,
the Dockers' Societies, the Good Templars, the
Bands of Mercy, groups of children, religious
fraternities, political associations, workmen's associations, the great army of labourers, and behind,
in still closer ranks, that vast assemblage of the

wretched who usually only emerge in gloomy hours of trouble. This incongruous crowd lined the way during the whole distance from the Oratory to the Cemetery. At several places on the road bands played funeral marches. When the hearse passed all this multitude, Protestants or Catholics, Socialists or revolutionaries, knelt or uncovered. It seemed as if, for one day, the two worlds separated by our materialistic and mercantile civilization clasped hands and were reconciled in a common sorrow above that coffin where slept Christ's servant.

Such were the obsequies of Henry Edward Manning, Cardinal Priest of the Holy Roman Church, of the title of St. Andrew and St. Gregory on the Cœlian Hill, Archbishop of Westminster, Catholic Primate of England. Our century has perhaps seen more pompous funerals, it has never seen a more touching one, made as they were by a whole people. Manning had no need of any other funeral oration.

I have tried to tell the story of his life; that long effort towards truth, that heroic sacrifice of all that is dear to man, that passion for certainty which flung him at the feet of the Infallible Church, and when there, at the feet of the Vicar of Jesus Christ, the incorruptible guardian of the trust of the Faith. I have tried also to describe that noble attempt to restore humanity to the Church, and to make the Church conscious of her mission of enfranchisement, of consolation and salvation to society as well as to individuals.

Before this great figure, the embodiment of austerity and love, of asceticism and charity, before the memory of this man who loved power, but only that he might consecrate it to the noblest uses, these words rise involuntarily to the lips— *Ecce sacerdos magnus !*

THE END

Richard Clay & Sons, Limited, London & Bungay.

21 BEDFORD STREET, W.C.

Telegraphic Address,
Sunlocks, London

A List of

Mr. William Heinemann's

Publications and

Announcements

*The Books mentioned in this List can
be obtained to order by any Book-
seller if not in stock, or will be sent
by the Publisher on receipt of the
published price and postage.*

August 1896.

Index of Authors

THE WORKS OF LORD BYRON.

EDITED BY WILLIAM ERNEST HENLEY.

IN TWELVE VOLUMES.

VOLUME I. LETTERS, 1804–1813.

To be followed by

VOLUMES II.–IV. LETTERS AND SPEECHES.

VOLUME V. HOURS OF IDLENESS, ENGLISH BARDS AND SCOTCH REVIEWERS.

VOLUME VI. CHILDE HAROLD.

Small cr. 8vo, price 5s. each.

Also an Edition limited to 150 sets for sa'e in Great Britain, printed on Van Gelder's handmade paper, price Six Guineas the set net.

It is agreed that Byron's Letters, public and private, with their abounding ease and spirit and charm, are among the best in English. It is thought that Byron's poetry has been long, and long enough, neglected, so that we are on the eve of, if not face to face with, a steady reaction in its favour: that, in fact, the true public has had enough of fluent minor lyrists and hide-bound (if superior) sonnetteers, and is disposed, in the natural course of things, to renew its contact with a great English poet, who was also a principal element in the æsthetic evolution of that Modern Europe which we know.

Hence this new Byron, which will present—for the first time since the Seventeen Volumes Edition (1833), long since out of print—a master-writer and a master-influence in decent and persuasive terms.

It is barely necessary to dwell on Mr. Henley's special qualifications for the task of editing and annotating the works of our poet.

THE CASTLES OF ENGLAND:

THEIR STORY AND STRUCTURE.

By SIR JAMES D. MACKENZIE, BART.

Dedicated by gracious permission to H.M. the Queen.

IN TWO VOLUMES.

Fully Illustrated and with many Plates.

Price £3 3s. net, on Subscription, to be raised on Publication.

It is the object of this work to record all that is known at the end of the nineteenth century with regard to every ancient castle in the kingdom, and it is believed that such a record must be welcome to all in whom the contemplation of these great historic monuments awakens not only admiration for their picturesque beauty, but also romantic speculation as to the stirring events which have happened there, and to the life once led within their walls.

There were in all about six hundred such castles of stone in England. Those that have vanished are frequently not the least interesting, and Fotheringay and Northampton conjure up memories as precious and heroic as if they were still standing. It has been the object of the author of this work to produce a Book of Reference in which will be found a trustworthy account of every fortress, defensible and castellated dwelling built from the Conquest to the reign of Henry VIII., including the forts or blockhouses built on the southern coast by that monarch.

Views of many of the castles are included in the work, and as much information as can be learned is given of their past history and condition. Plans are added to illustrate the position and defences of many of them, whereby their history and their structure may be the better understood.

The book will be divided into two volumes, the first containing twenty-seven Home, Southern and Midland Counties:

1. Kent.	10. Hants.	19. Warwick.
2. Sussex.	11. Wilts.	20. Gloucester.
3. Surrey.	12. Dorset.	21. Worcester.
4. Middlesex.	13. Essex.	22. Stafford.
5. Herts.	14. Suffolk.	23. Leicester.
6. Beds.	15 Norfolk.	24. Rutland.
7. Bucks.	16. Cambridge.	25. Lincoln.
8 Oxford.	17. Hunts.	26. Notts.
9. Berks.	18. Northants.	27. Derby.

The second containing thirteen Western and Northern Counties:

28. Cornwall.	32. Hereford.	37. Westmoreland.
29 Devon.	33. Shropshire.	38. Cumberland.
30. Somerset.	34. Cheshire.	39. Durham.
31. Monmouth.	35. Lancashire.	40. Northumberland.
	36. Yorkshire.	

The price to subscribers for the two volumes will be £3 3s. net.

If the present publication meets with popular approval, it is proposed to follow it up with the Castles of Scotland, Wales, and Ireland.

LIFE OF NELSON.

By ROBERT SOUTHEY.

A NEW EDITION

EDITED BY DAVID HANNAY.

Crown 8vo, Gilt, with Portrait.

SOUTHEY'S LIFE OF NELSON is an acknowledged masterpiece of literature. It can never cease to have value, even if it is at any future time
surpassed in its own qualities. Up to the present it has never been
equalled. While we are waiting for the appearance of a better Southey,
the old may well be published with a much-needed *apparatus criticus.*
The object of the new edition is to put forth the text, supported by
notes, which will make good the few oversights committed by Southey,
the passages in Nelson's life of which he had not heard, or which he,
influenced by highly honourable scruples, did not think fit to speak of
so soon after the hero's death, and while some of the persons concerned
were still living. A brief account will also be given of the naval officers,
and less famous soldiers or civilians mentioned, though it will not be
thought needful to tell the reader the already well-known facts concern-
ing Pitt, Sir John Moore, or Paoli. Emma Hamilton, of whom Southey
said only the little which was necessary to preserve his book from
downright falsity, will have her history told at what is now adequate
length. The much debated story of Nelson's actions at Naples will be
told from a point of view other than Southey's. It is not proposed
to write a new life of Nelson, but only to set forth the best of existing
biographies with necessary additions and corrections, as well as with
some comment on his qualities as a commander in naval warfare.

THE LIFE OF THE LATE
SIR JOSEPH BARNBY.

By W. H. SONLEY JOHNSTONE.

In One Volume, with Portraits, 8vo.

SIR JOSEPH BARNBY was a personality and an influence ; music was
only a part of him. He was an arduous worker, a brilliant talker, a
raconteur of merit, a good speaker, and a popular favourite in society.
The period through which he lived was one of the most important and
fruitful in the annals of English music, and Mr. Johnstone will receive
the assistance of composers and others in making this work as compre-
hensive as possible.

The main divisions will be : Music in England Half-a-Century Ago—
Early Life of Barnby—His Eton Career—His Albert Hall Career—As
Composer and Conductor—His Social and General Life—The Academy
and Guildhall.

𝔏iteratures of the 𝔚orld.

EDITED BY
EDMUND GOSSE.

M R. HEINEMANN begs to announce a Series of Short Histories of Ancient and Modern Literatures of the World, Edited by EDMUND GOSSE.

The following volumes are projected, and it is probable that they will be the first to appear :—

FRENCH LITERATURE.
BY EDWARD DOWDEN, D.C.L., LL.D., Professor of English Literature at the University of Dublin.

ANCIENT GREEK LITERATURE.
BY GILBERT G. A. MURRAY, M.A., Professor of Greek in the University of Glasgow.

ENGLISH LITERATURE.
BY THE EDITOR.

ITALIAN LITERATURE.
BY RICHARD GARNETT, C.B., LL.D., Keeper of Printed Books in the British Museum.

MODERN SCANDINAVIAN LITERATURE
BY DR. GEORG BRANDES, of Copenhagen.

JAPANESE LITERATURE.
BY WILLIAM GEORGE ASTON, M.A., C.M.G., late Acting Secretary at the British Legation at Tokio.

SPANISH LITERATURE.
BY J. FITZMAURICE-KELLY, Member of the Spanish Academy.

WILLIAM SHAKESPEARE:
A CRITICAL STUDY.

By GEORG BRANDES.

Translated from the Danish by WILLIAM ARCHER

In Two Volumes, demy 8vo.

Dr. Georg Brandes's "William Shakespeare" may best be called, perhaps, an exhaustive critical biography. Keeping fully abreast of the latest English and German researches and criticism, Dr. Brandes preserves that breadth and sanity of view which is apt to be sacrificed by the mere Shakespearologist. He places the poet in his political and literary environment, and studies each play not as an isolated phenomenon, but as the record of a stage in Shakespeare's spiritual history. Dr. Brandes has achieved German thoroughness without German heaviness, and has produced what must be regarded as a standard work.

ROBERT, EARL NUGENT:
A MEMOIR.

By CLAUD NUGENT.

In One Volume, demy 8vo, with a number of Portraits and other Illustrations.

A BOOK OF SCOUNDRELS
By CHARLES WHIBLEY.

In One Volume, crown 8vo, with a Frontispiece.

In "A Book of Scoundrels" are described the careers and achievements of certain notorious malefactors who have been chosen for their presentment on account of their style and picturesqueness. They are of all ages and several countries, and that variety may not be lacking, Cartouche and Peace, Moll Cutpurse and the Abbé Bruneau, come within the same covers. Where it has seemed convenient, the method of Plutarch is followed, and the style and method of two similar scoundrels are contrasted in a "parallel." Jack Shepherd in the tone-room of Newgate, reproduced from an old print, serves as a frontispiece.

IN CAP AND GOWN.
THREE CENTURIES OF CAMBRIDGE WIT.

EDITED BY CHARLES WHIBLEY.

Third Edition, with a New Introduction, crown 8vo.

SEVENTEENTH-CENTURY STUDIES.

A CONTRIBUTION TO THE HISTORY OF ENGLISH POETRY.

By EDMUND GOSSE,

Clark Lecturer on English Literature at the University of Cambridge.
A New Edition. Crown 8vo.

SPANISH PROTESTANTS IN THE SIXTEENTH CENTURY.

COMPILED FROM DR. WILKEN'S GERMAN WORK

By RACHEL E. CHALLICE.

WITH AN INTRODUCTION BY
THE MOST REV. LORD PLUNKET, ARCHBISHOP OF DUBLIN, D.D.,
And a Preface by THE REV. CANON FLEMING, B.D.

In One Volume.

UNDERCURRENTS OF THE SECOND EMPIRE.

By ALBERT D. VANDAM,

Author of "An Englishman in Paris" and "My Paris Note-book."
Demy 8vo, 10s. 6d.

"MADE IN GERMANY."

REPRINTED WITH ADDITIONS FROM *THE NEW REVIEW*.

By ERNEST E. WILLIAMS.

In One Volume. Crown 8vo, cloth, 2s. 6d.

The Industrial Supremacy of Great Britain has been long an axiomatic commonplace; it is fast turning into a myth.

These papers are not prompted by the Bimetallic League, nor by devotion to fair trade, nor by any of the economic schemes and doctrines which reformers are propounding for the cure of our commercial dry-rot. It is the Author's object to proceed on scientific lines, to collect and arrange the facts so that they may clearly show forth the causes, and point with inevitableness to the remedies, if and where there be any.

GENIUS AND DEGENERATION:

A PSYCHOLOGICAL STUDY.

By Dr. WILLIAM HIRSCH.

With an Introduction by Professor E. MENDEL.

Translated from the Second German Edition.

In One Volume, demy 8vo.

LETTERS OF
A COUNTRY VICAR.

Translated from the French of YVES LE QUERDEC.

By M. GORDON-HOLMES.

In One Volume, crown 8vo.

This translation of a work which, in the original, has evoked a quite exceptional measure of attention, will be welcomed for its vivid pictures of country life in France, and of the relations subsisting between Church and laity.

THE AGNOSTICISM OF THE
FUTURE.

FROM THE FRENCH OF

M. GUYAU.

In One Volume, 8vo.

THE BLACK RIDERS
VERSES.

By STEPHEN CRANE,

Author of "The Red Badge of Courage."

A 2

ANTONIO ALLEGRI DA CORREGIO: His Life, his
Friends, and his Time. By CORRADO RICCI, Director of the Royal Gallery, Parma. Translated by FLORENCE SIMMONDS. With 16 Photogravure Plates, 21 full-page Plates in Tint, and 190 Illustrations in the Text. In One Volume, imperial 8vo, £2 2s. net.

. *Also a special edition printed on Japanese vellum, limited to 100 copies, with duplicate plates on India paper. Price £12 12s. net.*

REMBRANDT: His Life, his Work, and his Time. By EMILE
MICHEL, Member of the Institute of France. Translated by FLORENCE SIMMONDS. Edited and Prefaced by FREDERICK WEDMORE. Second Edition, Enlarged, with 76 full-page Plates, and 250 Illustrations in the Text. In One Volume, Gilt top, or in Two Volumes, imperial 8vo, £2 2s. net.

. *A few copies of the EDITION DE LUXE of the First Edition, printed on Japanese vellum with India proof duplicates of the photogravures, are still on sale, price £12 12s. net.*

REMBRANDT. Seventeen of his Masterpieces from the collection of his Pictures in the Cassel Gallery. Reproduced in Photogravure by the Berlin Photographic Company. With an Essay by FREDERICK WEDMORE. In large portfolio 27½ inches × 20 inches.

The first twenty-five impressions of each plate are numbered and signed, and of these only fourteen are for sale in England at the net price of Twenty Guineas the set. The price of the impressions after the first twenty-five is Twelve Guineas net, per set.

MASTERPIECES OF GREEK SCULPTURE. A Series
of Essays on the History of Art. By ADOLF FURTWANGLER. Authorised Translation. Edited by EUGENIE SELLERS. With 19 full-page and 200 text Illustrations. In One Volume, imperial 8vo, £3 3s. net.

. *Also an EDITION DE LUXE on Japanese vellum, limited to 50 numbered copies in Two Volumes, price £10 10s. net.*

THE HOURS OF RAPHAEL, IN OUTLINE. Together
with the Ceiling of the Hall where they were originally painted. By MARY E. WILLIAMS. Folio, cloth, £2 2s. net.

A CATALOGUE OF THE ACCADEMIA DELLE
BELLE ARTI AT VENICE. With Biographical Notices of the Painters and Reproductions of some of their Works. Edited by E. M. KEARY. Crown 8vo, cloth, 2s. 6d. net; paper, 2s. net.

A CATALOGUE OF THE MUSEO DEL PRADO AT
MADRID. Compiled by F. LAWSON. In One Volume, crown 8vo.
[In preparation.

THE PAGET PAPERS. Diplomatic and other Correspondence of THE RIGHT HON. SIR ARTHUR PAGET, G.C.B., 1794-1807. With two Appendices, 1808 and 1828-1829. Arranged and Edited by his son, The Right Hon. SIR AUGUSTUS B. PAGET, G C.B., late Her Majesty's Ambassador in Vienna. With Notes by Mrs. J. R. GREEN. In Two Volumes, demy 8vo, with Portraits, 32s. net.

These volumes deal with the earlier Napoleonic Wars, and throw a new light on almost every phase of that most vital period of European history.

BROTHER AND SISTER. A Memoir and the Letters of ERNEST and HENRIETTE RENAN. Translated by Lady MARY LOYD. Demy 8vo, with Two Portraits in Photogravure, and Four Illustrations, 14s.

Mr. GLADSTONE has written to the publisher as follows : " I have read the whole of the Renan Memoirs, and have found them to be of peculiar and profound interest."

The Illustrated London News.—"One of the most exquisite memorials in all literature."

CHARLES GOUNOD. Autobiographical Reminiscences with Family Letters and Notes on Music. Translated by the Hon. W. HELY HUTCHINSON. Demy 8vo, with Portrait, 10s. 6d.

The Daily News—"Interwoven with many touching domestic details, it furnishes a continuous history of the dawn and development of his genius down to the period when his name had become familiar in all men's mouths."

STUDIES IN DIPLOMACY. By Count BENEDETTI, French Ambassador at the Court of Berlin. Demy 8vo, with a Portrait, 10s. 6d.

The Times.—"An important and authentic contribution to the history of a great crisis in the affairs of Europe."

AN AMBASSADOR OF THE VANQUISHED. Viscount Elie De Gontaut-Biron's Mission to Berlin, 1871-1877. From his Diaries and Memoranda. By the DUKE DE BROGLIE. Translated with Notes by ALBERT D. VANDAM, Author of "An Englishman in Paris." In One Volume, 8vo, 10s. 6d.

The Times.—"The real interest of the book consists in the new contributions which it makes to our knowledge of the dangerous crisis of 1875."

ANIMAL SYMBOLISM IN ECCLESIASTICAL ARCHITECTURE. By E. P. EVANS. With a Bibliography and Seventy-eight Illustrations, crown 8vo, 9s.

The Manchester Courier.—"A work of considerable learning. We have not often read a book that contains more quaint and unusual information, or is more closely packed with matter. It is very pleasant reading and may be commended to all who are interested in the by-paths of literature and art."

Great Lives and Events.

Uniformly bound in cloth, 6s. each volume.

A FRIEND OF THE QUEEN. Marie Antoinette and Count Fersen. From the French of PAUL GAULOT. Two Portraits.

The Times —" M. Gaulot's work tells, with new and authentic details, the romantic story of Count Fersen's devotion to Marie Antoinette, of his share in the celebrated Flight to Varennes and in many other well-known episodes of the unhappy Queen's life."

THE ROMANCE OF AN EMPRESS. Catherine II. of Russia. From the French of K. WALISZEWSKI. With a Portrait.

The Times.—" This book is based on the confessions of the Empress herself; it gives striking pictures of the condition of the contemporary Russia which she did so much to mould as well as to expand. . . . Few stories in history are more romantic than that of Catherine II. of Russia, with its mysterious incidents and thrilling episodes ; few characters present more curious problems."

THE STORY OF A THRONE. Catherine II. of Russia. From the French of K. WALISZEWSKI. With a Portrait.

The World.—" No novel that ever was written could compete with this historical monograph in absorbing interest."

NAPOLEON AND THE FAIR SEX. From the French of FRÉDÉRIC MASSON. With a Portrait.

The Daily Chronicle.—" The author shows that this side of Napoleon's life must be understood by those who would realize the manner of man he was."

ALFRED, LORD TENNYSON. A Study of His Life and Work. By ARTHUR WAUGH, B.A. Oxon. With Twenty Illustrations from Photographs specially taken for this Work. Five Portraits, and Facsimile of Tennyson's MS.

MEMOIRS OF THE PRINCE DE JOINVILLE. Translated from the French by Lady MARY LOYD. With 78 Illustrations from drawings by the Author.

THE NATURALIST OF THE SEA-SHORE. The Life of Philip Henry Gosse. By his son, EDMUND GOSSE, Hon. M.A., Trinity College, Cambridge. With a Portrait.

THE FAMILY LIFE OF HEINRICH HEINE. Illustrated by one hundred and twenty-two hitherto unpublished letters addressed by him to different members of his family. Edited by his nephew, Baron LUDWIG VON EMBDEN, and translated by CHARLES GODFREY LELAND. With 4 Portraits.

RECOLLECTIONS OF COUNT LEO TOLSTOY. Together with a Letter to the Women of France on the " Kreutzer Sonata." By C. A. BEHRS. Translated from the Russian by C. E. TURNER, English Lecturer in the University of St. Petersburg. With Portrait.

MY PARIS NOTE-BOOK. By ALBERT D. VANDAM, Author of "An Englishman in Paris." In One Volume, demy 8vo, price 6s.

EDMUND AND JULES DE GONCOURT. Letters and Leaves from their Journals. Selected. In Two Volumes, 8vo, with Eight Portraits, 32s.

ALEXANDER III. OF RUSSIA. By CHARLES LOWE, M.A., Author of "Prince Bismarck: an Historical Biography." Crown 8vo, with Portrait in Photogravure, 6s.

The Athenæum.—"A most interesting and valuable volume."

The Academy.—"Written with great care and strict impartiality."

PRINCE BISMARCK. An Historical Biography. By CHARLES LOWE, M.A. With Portraits. Crown 8vo, 6s.

VILLIERS DE L'ISLE ADAM: His Life and Works. From the French of VICOMTE ROBERT DU PONTAVICE DE HEUSSEY. By Lady MARY LOYD. With Portrait and Facsimile. Crown 8vo, cloth, 10s. 6d.

THE LIFE OF HENRIK IBSEN. By HENRIK JÆGER. Translated by CLARA BELL. With the Verse done into English from the Norwegian Original by EDMUND GOSSE. Crown 8vo, cloth, 6s.

RECOLLECTIONS OF MIDDLE LIFE. By FRANCISQUE SARCEY. Translated by E. L. CAREY. In One Volume, 8vo, with Portrait, 10s. 6d.

TWENTY-FIVE YEARS IN THE SECRET SERVICE. The Recollections of a Spy. By Major HENRI LE CARON. With New Preface. 8vo, boards, price 2s. 6d., or cloth, 3s. 6d.

⁎⁎ *The Library Edition, with Portraits and Facsimiles, 8vo, 14s., is still on sale.*

QUEEN JOANNA I. OF NAPLES, SICILY, AND JERUSALEM; Countess of Provence, Forcalquier, and Piedmont. An Essay on her Times. By ST. CLAIR BADDELEY. Imperial 8vo, with numerous Illustrations, 16s.

CHARLES III. OF NAPLES AND URBAN VI.; also CECCO D'ASCOLI, Poet, Astrologer, Physician. Two Historical Essays. By ST. CLAIR BADDELEY. With Illustrations, 8vo, cloth, 10s. 6d.

LETTERS OF SAMUEL TAYLOR COLERIDGE. Edited by ERNEST HARTLEY COLERIDGE. With 16 Portraits and Illustrations. In Two Volumes, demy 8vo, £1 12s.

DE QUINCEY MEMORIALS. Being Letters and other Records here first Published, with Communications from COLERIDGE, the WORDSWORTHS, HANNAH MORE, PROFESSOR WILSON, and others. Edited with Introduction, Notes, and Narrative, by ALEXANDER H. JAPP, LL.D., F.R.S.E. In Two Volumes, demy 8vo, cloth, with Portraits, 30s. net.

MEMOIRS. By CHARLES GODFREY LELAND (HANS BREIT-MANN). Second Edition. In One Volume, 8vo, with Portrait, price 7s. 6d.

LETTERS OF A BARITONE. By FRANCIS WALKER. Square crown 8vo, 5s.

THE LOVE LETTERS OF MR. H. AND MISS R. 1775–1779. Edited by GILBERT BURGESS. Square crown 8vo, 5s.

PARADOXES. By MAX NORDAU, Author of "Degeneration," "Conventional Lies of our Civilisation," &c. Translated by J. R. McILRAITH. Demy 8vo, 17s. *net.* With an Introduction by the Author written for this Edition.

CONVENTIONAL LIES OF OUR CIVILIZATION. By MAX NORDAU, author of "Degeneration." Second English Edition. Demy 8vo, 17s. net.

DEGENERATION. By MAX NORDAU. Ninth English Edition. Demy 8vo, 17s. net.

THE PROSE WORKS OF HEINRICH HEINE. Translated by CHARLES GODFREY LELAND, M.A., F.R.L.S. (HANS BREITMANN). In Eight Volumes.

The Library Edition, in crown 8vo, cloth, at 5s. per Volume. Each Volume of this edition is sold separately. The Cabinet Edition, in special binding, boxed, price £2 10s. the set. The Large Paper Edition, limited to 50 Numbered Copies, price 15s. per Volume net, will only be supplied to subscribers for the Complete Work.

> I. FLORENTINE NIGHTS, SCHNABELEWOPSKI, THE RABBI OF BACHARACH, and SHAKE-SPEARE'S MAIDENS AND WOMEN.
>
> II., III. PICTURES OF TRAVEL. 1823–1828.
>
> IV. THE SALON. Letters on Art, Music, Popular Life, and Politics.
>
> V., VI. GERMANY.
>
> VII., VIII. FRENCH AFFAIRS. Letters from Paris 1832, and Lutetia.

THE POSTHUMOUS WORKS OF THOMAS DE QUINCEY. Edited, with Introduction and Notes from the Author's Original MSS., by ALEXANDER H. JAPP, LL.D., F.R.S.E., &c. Crown 8vo, cloth, 6s. each.

> I. SUSPIRIA DE PROFUNDIS. With other Essays.
>
> II. CONVERSATION AND COLERIDGE. With other Essays.

CRITICAL KIT-KATS. By EDMUND GOSSE, Hon. M.A. of Trinity College, Cambridge. Crown 8vo, buckram, gilt top, 7s. 6d.

QUESTIONS AT ISSUE. Essays. By EDMUND GOSSE. Crown 8vo, buckram, gilt top, 7s. 6d.
. *A Limited Edition on Large Paper,* 25s. net.

GOSSIP IN A LIBRARY. By EDMUND GOSSE, Author of "Northern Studies," &c. Third Edition. Crown 8vo, buckram, gilt top, 7s. 6d.
. *A Limited Edition on Large Paper,* 25s. net.

CORRECTED IMPRESSIONS. Essays on Victorian Writers. By GEORGE SAINTSBURY. Crown 8vo, gilt top, 7s. 6d.

ANIMA POETÆ. From the unpublished note-books of SAMUEL TAYLOR COLERIDGE. Edited by ERNEST HARTLEY COLERIDGE. In One Volume, crown 8vo, 7s. 6d.

ESSAYS. By ARTHUR CHRISTOPHER BENSON, of Eton College. In One Volume, crown 8vo, buckram, 7s. 6d.

THE CHITRAL CAMPAIGN. A Narrative of Events in Chitral, Swat, and Bajour. By H. C. THOMSON. With over 50 Illustrations reproduced from Photographs, and important Diagrams and Map. Second Edition in One Volume, demy 8vo, 14s. net.

WITH THE ZHOB FIELD FORCE, 1890. By Captain CRAWFORD McFALL, K.O.Y.L.I. In One Volume, demy 8vo, with Illustrations, 18s.

THE LAND OF THE MUSKEG. By H. SOMERS SOMERSET. Second Edition. In One Volume, demy 8vo, with Maps and over 100 Illustrations, 280 pp., 14s. net.

ACTUAL AFRICA; or, The Coming Continent. A Tour of Exploration. By FRANK VINCENT, Author of "The Land of the White Elephant." With Map and over 100 Illustrations, demy 8vo, cloth, price 24s.

COREA, OR CHO-SEN, THE LAND OF THE MORN- ING CALM. By A. HENRY SAVAGE-LANDOR. With 38 Illustrations from Drawings by the Author, and a Portrait, demy 8vo, 18s.

THE LITTLE MANX NATION. (Lectures delivered at the Royal Institution, 1891.) By HALL CAINE, Author of "The Bondman," "The Scapegoat," &c. Crown 8vo, cloth, 3s. 6d.; paper, 2s. 6d.

NOTES FOR THE NILE. Together with a Metrical Rendering of the Hymns of Ancient Egypt and of the Precepts of Ptah-hotep (the oldest book in the world). By HARDWICKE D. RAWNSLEY, M.A. Imperial 16mo, cloth, 5s.

DENMARK: its History, Topography, Language, Literature. Fine Arts, Social Life, and Finance. Edited by H. WEITEMEYER. Demy 8vo, cloth, with Map, 12s. 6d.
. *Dedicated, by permission, to H.R.H. the Princess of Wales.*

THE REALM OF THE HABSBURGS. By SIDNEY WHITMAN, Author of "Imperial Germany." In One Volume, crown 8vo, 7s. 6d.

IMPERIAL GERMANY. A Critical Study of Fact and Character. By SIDNEY WHITMAN. New Edition, Revised and Enlarged. Crown 8vo, cloth, 2s. 6d.; paper, 2s.

THE CANADIAN GUIDE-BOOK. Part I. The Tourist's and Sportsman's Guide to Eastern Canada and Newfoundland, including full descriptions of Routes, Cities, Points of Interest, Summer Resorts, Fishing Places, &c., in Eastern Ontario, The Muskoka Dis'rict, The St. Lawrence Region, The Lake St. John Country, The Maritime Provinces, Prince Edward Island, and Newfoundland. With an Appendix giving Fish and Game Laws, and Official Lists of Trout and Salmon Rivers and their Lessees. By CHARLES G. D. ROBERTS, Professor of English Literature in King's College, Windsor, N.S. With Maps and many Illustrations. Crown 8vo, limp cloth, 6s.

THE CANADIAN GUIDE-BOOK. Part II. WESTERN CANADA. Including the Peninsula and Northern Regions of Ontario, the Canadian Shores of the Great Lakes, the Lake of the Woods Region, Manitoba and "The Great North-West," The Canadian Rocky Mountains and National Park, British Columbia, and Vancouver Island. By ERNEST INGERSOLL. With Maps and many Illustrations. Crown 8vo, limp cloth, 6s.

THE GUIDE-BOOK TO ALASKA AND THE NORTH- WEST COAST, including the Shores of Washington, British Columbia, South-Eastern Alaska, the Aleutian and the Seal Islands, the Behring and the Arctic Coasts. By E. R. SCIDMORE. With Maps and many Illustrations. Crown 8vo, limp cloth, 6s.

THE GENESIS OF THE UNITED STATES. A Narrative of the Movement in England, 1605–1616, which resulted in the Plantation of North America by Englishmen, disclosing the Contest between England and Spain for the Possession of the Soil now occupied by the United States of America; set forth through a series of Historical Manuscripts now first printed, together with a Re-issue of Rare Contemporaneous Tracts, accompanied by Bibliographical Memoranda, Notes, and Brief Biographies. Collected, Arranged, and Edited by ALEXANDER BROWN, F.R.H.S. With 100 Portraits, Maps, and Plans. In Two Volumes, royal 8vo, buckram, £3 13s. 6d. net.

IN THE TRACK OF THE SUN. Readings from the Diary of a Globe-Trotter. By FREDERICK DIODATI THOMPSON. With many Illustrations by Mr. HARRY FENN and from Photographs. In One Volume, 4to, 25s.

THE GREAT WAR OF 189—. A Forecast. By Rear-Admiral COLOMB, Col. MAURICE, R.A., Captain MAUDE, ARCHIBALD FORBES, CHARLES LOWE, D. CHRISTIE MURRAY, and F. SCUDAMORE. Second Edition. In One Volume, large 8vo, with numerous Illustrations, 6s.

THE COMING TERROR. And other Essays and Letters. By ROBERT BUCHANAN. Second Edition. Demy 8vo, cloth, 12s. 6d.

AS OTHERS SAW HIM. A Retrospect, A.D. 54. In One Volume. Crown 8vo, gilt top 6s.

ISRAEL AMONG THE NATIONS. Translated from the French of ANATOLE LEROY-BEAULIEU, Member of the Institute of France. In One Volume, crown 8vo, 7s. 6d.

THE JEW AT HOME. Impressions of a Summer and Autumn Spent with Him in Austria and Russia. By JOSEPH PENNELL. With Illustrations by the Author. 4to, cloth, 5s.

THE NEW EXODUS. A Study of Israel in Russia. By HAROLD FREDERIC. Demy 8vo, Illustrated, 16s.

STUDIES OF RELIGIOUS HISTORY. By ERNEST RENAN, late of the French Academy. In One Volume, 8vo, 7s. 6d

THE ARBITRATOR'S MANUAL. Under the London Chamber of Arbitration. Being a Practical Treatise on the Power and Duties of an Arbitrator, with the Rules and Procedure of the Court of Arbitration, and the Forms. By JOSEPH SEYMOUR SALAMAN, Author of "Trade Marks," &c. Fcap. 8vo, 3s. 6d.

MANNERS, CUSTOMS, AND OBSERVANCES: Their Origin and Signification. By LEOIOLD WAGNER. Crown 8vo, 6s.

A COMMENTARY ON THE WORKS OF HENRIK IBSEN. By HJALMAR HJORTH BOYESEN, Author of "Goethe and Schiller," "Essays on German Literature," &c. Crown 8vo, cloth, 7s. 6d. net.

THE LABOUR MOVEMENT IN AMERICA. By RICHARD T. ELY, Ph.D., Associate in Political Economy, John Hopkins University. Crown 8vo, cloth, 5s.

THE PASSION PLAY AT OBERAMMERGAU, 1890. By F. W. FARRAR, D.D., F.R.S., Dean of Canterbury, &c. &c. 4to, cloth, 2s. 6d.

THE WORD OF THE LORD UPON THE WATERS. Sermons read by His Imperial Majesty the Emperor of Germany, while at Sea on his Voyages to the Land of the Midnight Sun. Composed by Dr. RICHTER, Army Chaplain, and Translated from the German by JOHN R. McILRAITH. 4to, cloth, 2s. 6d.

THE KINGDOM OF GOD IS WITHIN YOU. Christianity not as a Mystic Religion but as a New Theory of Life. By Count LEO TOLSTOY. Translated from the Russian by CONSTANCE GARNETT. Popular Edition in One Volume, cloth, 2s. 6d.

THE SPINSTER'S SCRIP. As Compiled by GECIL
RAYNOR. Narrow crown 8vo, limp cloth, 2s. 6d.

THE POCKET IBSEN. A Collection of some of the Master's
best known Dramas, condensed, revised, and slightly rearranged for the
benefit of the Earnest Student. By F. ANSTEY, Author of " Vice Versa,"
" Voces Populi," &c. With Illustrations, reproduced by permission,
from *Punch*, and a new Frontispiece, by BERNARD PARTRIDGE. New
Edition. 16mo, cloth, 3s. 6d. ; or paper, 2s. 6d.

FROM WISDOM COURT. By HENRY SETON MERRIMAN
and STEPHEN GRAHAM TALLENTYRE. With 30 Illustrations by
E. COURBOIN. Crown 8vo, cloth, 3s. 6d. ; or picture boards, 2s.

THE OLD MAIDS' CLUB. By I. ZANGWILL, Author of
" Children of the Ghetto," &c. Illustrated by F. H. TOWNSEND. Crown
8vo, cloth, 3s. 6d. ; or picture boards, 2s.

WOMAN—THROUGH A MAN'S EYEGLASS. By
MALCOLM C. SALAMAN. With Illustrations by DUDLEY HARDY. Crown
8vo, cloth, 3s. 6d. ; or picture boards, 2s.

STORIES OF GOLF. Collected by WILLIAM KNIGHT and
T. T. OLIPHANT. With Rhymes on Golf by various hands ; also Shakespeare on Golf, &c. *Enlarged Edition.* Fcap. 8vo, cloth, 2s. 6d.

THE ROSE : A Treatise on the Cultivation, History, Family
Characteristics, &c., of the various Groups of Roses. With Accurate
Description of the Varieties now Generally Grown. By H. B. ELL-
WANGER. With an Introduction by GEORGE H. ELLWANGER. 12mo,
cloth, 5s.

THE GARDEN'S STORY; or, Pleasures and Trials of an
Amateur Gardener. By G. H. ELLWANGER. With an Introduction by the
Rev. C. WOLLEY DOD. 12mo, cloth, with Illustrations, 5s.

THE GENTLE ART OF MAKING ENEMIES. As
pleasingly exemplified in many instances, wherein the serious ones of
this earth, carefully exasperated, have been prettily spurred on to
indiscretions and unseemliness, while overcome by an undue sense
of right. By J. M'NEILL WHISTLER. *A New Edition.* Post 4to,
half cloth, 10s. 6d.

. A few copies of the large paper issue of the first edition remain, price
£1 11s. 6d. *net.*

LITTLE JOHANNES. By F. VAN EEDEN. Translated from
the Dutch by CLARA BELL. With an Introduction by ANDREW LANG.
In One Volume, 16mo, cloth, silver top, 3s. net.

GIRLS AND WOMEN. By E. CHESTER. Post 8vo, cloth,
2s. 6d., or gilt extra, 3s. 6d.

Dramatic Literature.

THE PLAYS OF W. E. HENLEY AND R. L. STEVEN-SON: — DEACON BRODIE; BEAU AUSTIN; ADMIRAL GUINEA; MACAIRE. Crown 8vo, cloth. An Edition of 250 copies only, 10s. 6d. net.

LITTLE EYOLF. A Play in Three Acts. By HENRIK IBSEN. Translated from the Norwegian by WILLIAM ARCHER. Small 4to, cloth, with Portrait, 5s.

THE MASTER BUILDER. A Play in Three Acts. By HENRIK IBSEN. Translated from the Norwegian by EDMUND GOSSE and WILLIAM ARCHER. Small 4to, with Portrait, 5s. Popular Edition, paper, 1s. Also a Limited Large Paper Edition, 21s. net.

HEDDA GABLER: A Drama in Four Acts. By HENRIK IBSEN. Translated from the Norwegian by EDMUND GOSSE. Small 4to, cloth, with Portrait, 5s. Vaudeville Edition, paper, 1s. Also a Limited Large Paper Edition, 21s. net.

BRAND: A Dramatic Poem in Five Acts. By HENRIK IBSEN. Translated in the original metres, with an Introduction and Notes, by C. H. HERFORD. Small 4to, cloth, 7s. 6d.

HANNELE: A DREAM-POEM. By GERHART HAUPT-MANN. Translated by WILLIAM ARCHER. Small 4to, with Portrait, 5s.

THE PRINCESSE MALEINE: A Drama in Five Acts (Translated by GERARD HARRY), and THE INTRUDER: A Drama in One Act. By MAURICE MAETERLINCK. With an Introduction by HALL CAINE, and a Portrait of the Author. Small 4to, cloth, 5s.

THE FRUITS OF ENLIGHTENMENT: A Comedy in Four Acts. By Count LYOF TOLSTOY. Translated from the Russian by E. J. DILLON. With Introduction by A. W. PINERO. Small 4to, with Portrait, 5s.

KING ERIK. A Tragedy. By EDMUND GOSSE. A Re-issue, with a Critical Introduction by Mr. THEODORE WATTS. Fcap. 8vo, boards, 5s. net.

THE PIPER OF HAMELIN. A Fantastic Opera in Two Acts. By ROBERT BUCHANAN. With Illustrations by HUGH THOMSON. 4to, cloth, 2s. 6d. net.

THE SIN OF ST. HULDA. A Play. By J. STUART OGILVIE. Fcap. 8vo, paper, 1s.

HYPATIA. A Play in Four Acts. Founded on CHARLES KINGSLEY'S Novel. By G. STUART OGILVIE. With Frontispiece by J. D. BATTEN. Crown 8vo, cloth, printed in Red and Black, 2s. 6d. net.

THE DRAMA: ADDRESSES. By HENRY IRVING. With Portrait by J. McN. WHISTLER. Second Edition. Fcap. 8vo, 3s. 6d.

SOME INTERESTING FALLACIES OF THE Modern Stage. An Address delivered to the Playgoers' Club at St. James's Hall, on Sunday, 6th December, 1891. By HERBERT BEERBOHM TREE. Crown 8vo, sewed, 6d. net.

THE PLAYS OF ARTHUR W. PINERO. With Introductory Notes by MALCOLM C. SALAMAN. 16mo, paper covers, 1s. 6d.; or cloth, 2s. 6d. each.

I. THE TIMES.	VII. DANDY DICK.
II. THE PROFLIGATE.	VIII. SWEET LAVENDER.
III. THE CABINET MINISTER.	IX. THE SCHOOL-MISTRESS.
IV. THE HOBBY HORSE.	X. THE WEAKER SEX.
V. LADY BOUNTIFUL.	XI. THE AMAZONS.
VI. THE MAGISTRATE.	

THE NOTORIOUS MRS. EBBSMITH. A Drama in Four Acts. By ARTHUR W. PINERO. Small 4to, cloth, 2s. 6d.; paper, 1s. 6d.

THE SECOND MRS. TANQUERAY. A Play in Four Acts. By ARTHUR W. PINERO. Small 4to, cloth, with a new Portrait of the Author, 5s. Also Cheap Edition, uniform with "The Notorious Mrs. Ebbsmith." Cloth, 2s. 6d.: paper, 1s. 6d.

THE BENEFIT OF THE DOUBT. By ARTHUR W. PINERO. Small 4to, cloth, 2s. 6d. : paper, 1s. 6d.

Poetry.

ON VIOL AND FLUTE. By EDMUND GOSSE. f cap. 8vo, with Frontispiece and Tailpiece, price 3s. 6d. net.

FIRDAUSI IN EXILE, and other Poems. By EDMUND GOSSE. Fcap. 8vo, with Frontispiece, price 3s. 6d. net.

IN RUSSET AND SILVER. POEMS. By EDMUND GOSSE. Author of "Gossip in a Library," &c. Crown 8vo, buckram, gilt top, 6s.

THE POETRY OF PATHOS AND DELIGHT. From the Works of COVENTRY PATMORE. Passages selected by ALICE MEYNELL. With a Photogravure Portrait from an Oil Painting by JOHN SARGENT, A.R.A. Fcap. 8vo, 5s.

A CENTURY OF GERMAN LYRICS. Translated from the German by KATE FREILIGRATH KROEKER. Fcap. 8vo, rough edges, 3s. 6d.

LOVE SONGS OF ENGLISH POETS, 1500–1800. With Notes by RALPH H. CAINE. Fcap. 8vo, rough edges, 3s. 6d.
. *Large Paper Edition, limited to* 100 *Copies,* 10s. 6d. *net.*

IVY AND PASSION FLOWER: Poems. By GERARD BENDALL, Author of "Estelle," &c. &c. 12mo, cloth, 3s. 6d.
Scotsman.—"Will be read with pleasure."
Musical World.—"The poems are delicate specimens of art, graceful and polished."

VERSES. By GERTRUDE HALL. 12mo, cloth, 3s. 6d.
Manchester Guardian.—"Will be welcome to every lover of poetry who takes it up."

IDYLLS OF WOMANHOOD. By C. AMY DAWSON. Fcap. 8vo, gilt top, 5s.

TENNYSON'S GRAVE. By ST. CLAIR BADDELEY. 8vo, paper, 1s.

Science and Education.

MOVEMENT. Translated from the French of E. MAREY. By ERIC PRITCHARD, M.A., M.B., Oxon. In One Volume, crown 8vo, with 170 Illustrations, 7s. 6d.

A popular and scientific treatise on movement, dealing chiefly with the locomotion of men, animals, birds, fish, and insects. A large number of the Illustrations are from instantaneous photographs.

ARABIC AUTHORS: A Manual of Arabian History and Literature. By F. F. ARBUTHNOT, M.R.A.S., Author of "Early Ideas," "Persian Portraits," &c. 8vo, cloth, 5s.

THE SPEECH OF MONKEYS. By Professor R. L. GARNER. Crown 8vo, 7s. 6d.

Heinemann's Scientific Handbooks.

THE BIOLOGICAL PROBLEM OF TO-DAY: Preformation or Epigenesis? Authorised Translation from the German of Prof. Dr. OSCAR HERTWIG, of the University of Berlin. By P. CHALMERS MITCHELL, M.A., Oxon. With a Preface by the Translator. Crown 8vo. 3s. 6d.

MANUAL OF BACTERIOLOGY. By A. B. GRIFFITHS, Ph.D., F.R.S. (Edin.), F.C.S. Crown 8vo, cloth, Illustrated. 7s. 6d.

Pharmaceutical Journal.—"The subject is treated more thoroughly and completely than in any similar work published in this country."

MANUAL OF ASSAYING GOLD, SILVER, COPPER, and Lead Ores. By WALTER LEE BROWN, B.Sc. Revised, Corrected, and considerably Enlarged, with a chapter on the Assaying of Fuel, &c. By A. B. GRIFFITHS, Ph.D., F.R.S. (Edin.), F.C.S. Crown 8vo, cloth, Illustrated, 7s. 6d.

Colliery Guardian.—"A delightful and fascinating book."

Financial World.—"The most complete and practical manual on everything which concerns assaying of all which have come before us."

GEODESY. By J. HOWARD GORE. Crown 8vo, cloth, Illustrated, 5s.

St. James's Gazette.—"The book may be safely recommended to those who desire to acquire an accurate knowledge of Geodesy."

Science Gossip.—"It is the best we could recommend to all geodetic students. It is full and clear, thoroughly accurate, and up to date in all matters of earth-measurements."

THE PHYSICAL PROPERTIES OF GASES. By ARTHUR L. KIMBALL, of the John Hopkins University. Crown 8vo, cloth, Illustrated, 5s.

Chemical News.—"The man of culture who wishes for a general and accurate acquaintance with the physical properties of gases, will find in Mr. Kimball's work just what he requires."

HEAT AS A FORM OF ENERGY. By Professor R. H. THURSTON, of Cornell University. Crown 8vo, cloth, Illustrated, 5s.

Manchester Examiner.—"Bears out the character of its predecessors for careful and correct statement and deduction under the light of the most recent discoveries."

The Great Educators.

A Series of Volumes by Eminent Writers, presenting in their entirety "A Biographical History of Education."

The Times.—"A Series of Monographs on 'The Great Educators' should prove of service to all who concern themselves with the history, theory, and practice of education."

The Speaker.—"There is a promising sound about the title of Mr. Heinemann's new series, 'The Great Educators.' It should help to allay the hunger and thirst for knowledge and culture of the vast multitude of young men and maidens which our educational system turns out yearly, provided at least with appetite for instruction."

Each subject will form a complete volume, crown 8vo, 5s.

Now ready.

ARISTOTLE, and the Ancient Educational Ideals. By THOMAS DAVIDSON, M.A., LL.D.

The Times.—"A very readable sketch of a very interesting subject."

LOYOLA, and the Educational System of the Jesuits. By REV. THOMAS HUGHES, S.J.

ALCUIN, and the Rise of the Christian Schools. By Professor ANDREW F. WEST, Ph.D.

FROEBEL, and Education by Self-Activity. By H. COURTHOPE BOWEN, M.A.

ABELARD, and the Origin and Early History of Universities. By JULES GABRIEL COMPAYRÉ, Professor in the Faculty of Toulouse.

HERBART AND THE HERBARTIANS. By Prof. DE GARMO.

In preparation.

ROUSSEAU; and, Education according to Nature. By PAUL H. HANUS.

HORACE MANN, and Public Education in the United States. By NICHOLAS MURRAY BUTLER, Ph.D.

THOMAS and MATTHEW ARNOLD, and their Influence on Education. By J. G. FITCH, LL.D., Her Majesty's Inspector of Schools.

PESTALOZZI; or, the Friend and Student of Children.

Forthcoming Fiction.

THE OTHER HOUSE. By HENRY JAMES. In Two Volumes.

ON THE FACE OF THE WATERS. By FLORA ANNIE STEEL.

LIFE THE ACCUSER. By E. F. BROOKE, Author of "A Superfluous Woman." In Three Volumes.

THE LITTLE REGIMENT. By STEPHEN CRANE. In One Volume.

THE CAPTAIN OF THE PARISH. By JOHN QUINE. In One Volume.

A COURT INTRIGUE. By BASIL THOMSON. In One Volume.

A NEW NOVEL by SARAH GRAND.

SAINT IVES. By ROBERT LOUIS STEVENSON. In One Volume.

A NEW NOVEL by HALL CAINE. In One Volume.

THE FOURTH NAPOLEON. By CHARLES BENHAM. In One Volume.

THE MAN OF STRAW. By E. W. PUGH. In One Volume.

CHUN-TI-KUNG. By CLAUDE REES. In One Volume, 6s.

BELOW THE SALT. By C. E. RAIMOND. In One Volume.

McCLEOD OF THE CAMERONS. By M. HAMILTON. In One Volume.

YEKL. A Tale of the New York Ghetto. By ABRAHAM CAHN. In One Volume.

THE GADFLY. By E. L. VOYNICH. In One Volume.

ANDREA. By PERCY WHITE. In One Volume.

Popular 6s. Novels.

THE FOLLY OF EUSTACE. By ROBERT HICHENS.
Crown 8vo, cloth, 6s.

AN IMAGINATIVE MAN. By ROBERT HICHENS. Crown
8vo, cloth, 6s.

THE ELEVENTH COMMANDMENT. By HALLIWELL
SUTCLIFFE. Crown 8vo, cloth, 6s.

ILLUMINATION. By HAROLD FREDERIC. Crown 8vo,
cloth, 6s.

HERBERT VANLENNERT. By C. F. KEARY. Crown
8vo, cloth, 6s.

CORRUPTION. By PERCY WHITE. Crown 8vo, cloth, 6s.

MR. BAILEY MARTIN. By PERCY WHITE. A New
Edition, uniform with "Corruption." Crown 8vo, with portrait, cloth, 6s

A SELF-DENYING ORDINANCE. By M. HAMILTON.
Crown 8vo, cloth, 6s.

THE MALADY OF THE CENTURY. By MAX NORDAU.
Crown 8vo, cloth, 6s.

A COMEDY OF SENTIMENT. By MAX NORDAU. Crown
8vo, cloth, 6s.

THE ISLAND OF DOCTOR MOREAU. By H. G. WELLS.
In One Volume. Crown 8vo.

STORIES FOR NINON. By ÉMILE ZOLA. Crown 8vo,
with a portrait by Will Rothenstein. Cloth, 6s.

THE YEARS THAT THE LOCUST HATH EATEN.
By ANNIE E. HOLDSWORTH. Crown 8vo, cloth, 6s.

IN HASTE AND AT LEISURE. By Mrs. LYNN LINTON.
Author of "Joshua Davidson," &c. Crown 8vo, cloth, 6s.

THE WORLD AND A MAN. By Z. Z. Cr. 8vo, cloth. 6s.

A DRAMA IN DUTCH. By Z. Z. Crown 8vo, cloth, 6s.

BENEFITS FORGOT. By WOLCOTT BALESTIER. A New
Edition. Crown 8vo, cloth, 6s.

A PASTORAL PLAYED OUT. By M. L. PENDERED.
Crown 8vo, cloth, 6s.

CHIMÆRA. By F. MABEL ROBINSON, Author of "Mr. Butler's
Ward," &c. Crown 8vo, cloth, 6s.

MISS GRACE OF ALL SOULS'. By W. EDWARDS TIRE-
BUCK. Crown 8vo, cloth, 6s.

A SUPERFLUOUS WOMAN. Crown 8vo, 6s.

TRANSITION. By the Author of "A Superfluous Woman."
Crown 8vo, cloth, 6s.

popular 6s. Novels.

WITHOUT SIN. By MARTIN J. PRITCHARD. Crown 8vo, cloth. 6s.

EMBARRASSMENTS. By HENRY JAMES. Crown 8vo, cloth. 6s.

TERMINATIONS. By HENRY JAMES. Second Edition. Crown 8vo, cloth, 6s.

THE FAILURE OF SIBYL FLETCHER. By ADELINE SERGEANT. Crown 8vo, cloth. 6s.

OUT OF DUE SEASON. By ADELINE SERGEANT. Crown 8vo, cloth, 6s.

SENTIMENTAL STUDIES. By HUBERT CRACKANTHORPE. Crown 8vo, cloth 6s.

THE EBB-TIDE. By ROBERT LOUIS STEVENSON and LLOYD OSBOURNE. Crown 8vo, cloth, 6s.

THE MANXMAN. By HALL CAINE. Crown 8vo, cloth, 6s.

THE BONDMAN. A New Saga. By HALL CAINE. Crown 8vo, cloth, 6s.

THE SCAPEGOAT. By HALL CAINE. Author of "The Bondman," &c. Crown 8vo, cloth, 6s.

ELDER CONKLIN; and other Stories. By FRANK HARRIS. 8vo, cloth, 6s.

THE HEAVENLY TWINS. By SARAH GRAND, Author of "Ideala," &c. Crown 8vo, cloth, 6s.

IDEALA. By SARAH GRAND, Author of "The Heavenly Twins." Crown 8vo, cloth, 6s.

OUR MANIFOLD NATURE. By SARAH GRAND. With a Portrait of the Author. Crown 8vo, cloth, 6s.

THE STORY OF A MODERN WOMAN. By ELLA HEPWORTH DIXON. Crown 8vo, cloth, 6s.

AT THE GATE OF SAMARIA. By W. J. LOCKE. Crown 8vo, cloth, 6s.

A DAUGHTER OF THIS WORLD. By F. BATTERSHALL. Crown 8vo, cloth, 6s.

THE LAST SENTENCE. By MAXWELL GRAY, Author of "The Silence of Dean Maitland," &c. Crown 8vo, cloth, 6s

THE POTTER'S THUMB. By F. A. STEEL, Author of "From the Five Rivers," &c. Crown 8vo, cloth, 6s.

FROM THE FIVE RIVERS. By FLORA ANNIE STEEL. Author of "Miss Stuart's Legacy." Crown 8vo, cloth, 6s.

RELICS. Fragments of a Life. By FRANCES MACNAB. Crown 8vo, cloth, 6s.

Popular 6s. Novels.

THE MASTER. By I. ZANGWILL. With Portrait. Crown 8vo, cloth, 6s.

CHILDREN OF THE GHETTO. By I. ZANGWILL, Author of "The Old Maids' Club," &c. New Edition, with Glossary Crown 8vo, cloth, 6s.

THE PREMIER AND THE PAINTER. A Fantastic Romance. By I. ZANGWILL and LOUIS COWEN. Third Edition. Crown 8vo, cloth, 6s.

THE KING OF SCHNORRERS, GROTESQUES AND FANTASIES. By I. ZANGWILL. With over Ninety Illustrations. Crown 8vo, cloth, 6s.

THE RECIPE FOR DIAMONDS. By C. J. CUTCLIFFE HYNE. Crown 8vo, cloth, 6s.

THE DANCER IN YELLOW. By W. E. NORRIS. Crown 8vo, cloth. 6s.

A VICTIM OF GOOD LUCK. By W. E. NORRIS, Author of "Matrimony," &c. Crown 8vo, cloth. 6s.

THE COUNTESS RADNA. By W. E. NORRIS, Author of "Matrimony," &c. Crown 8vo, cloth, 6s.

THE NAULAHKA. A Tale of West and East. By RUDYARD KIPLING and WOLCOTT BALESTIER. Second Edition. Crown 8vo, cloth, 6s.

A BATTLE AND A BOY. By BLANCHE WILLIS HOWARD. With Thirty-nine Illustrations by A. MAC-NIELL-BARBOUR. Crown 8vo, cloth gilt, 6s.

Five Shilling Volumes.

THE ATTACK ON THE MILL. By ÉMILE ZOLA. With Twenty-one Illustrations, and Five exquisitely printed Coloured Plates, from original drawings by E. COURBOIN. In One Volume, 4to, 5s.

THE SECRET OF NARCISSE. By EDMUND GOSSE. Crown 8vo, buckram, 5s.

VANITAS. By VERNON LEE, Author of "Hauntings," &c. Crown 8vo, cloth, 5s.

Two Shillings and Sixpence.

THE TIME MACHINE. By H. G. WELLS. Cloth, 2s. 6d.; paper, 1s. 6d.

THE DOMINANT SEVENTH: A Musical Story. By KATE ELIZABETH CLARKE. Crown 8vo, cloth, 2s. 6d.

The Pioneer Series.

12mo, cloth, 3s. net; or, paper covers, 2s. 6d. net.

The Athenæum.—"If this series keeps up to the present high level of interest, novel readers will have fresh cause for gratitude to Mr. Heinemann."

The Daily Telegraph.—"Mr. Heinemann's genial nursery of up-to-date romance."

The Observer.—"The smart Pioneer Series."

The Manchester Courier.—"The Pioneer Series promises to be as original as many other of Mr. Heinemann's ventures."

The Glasgow Herald.—"This very clever series."

The Sheffield Telegraph.—"The refreshingly original Pioneer Series."

Black and White.—"The brilliant Pioneer Series."

The Liverpool Mercury.—"Each succeeding issue of the Pioneer Series has a character of its own and a special attractiveness."

JOANNA TRAILL, SPINSTER. By ANNIE E. HOLDSWORTH.

GEORGE MANDEVILLE'S HUSBAND. By C. E. RAIMOND.

THE WINGS OF ICARUS. By LAURENCE ALMA TADEMA.

THE GREEN CARNATION. By ROBERT HICHENS.

AN ALTAR OF EARTH. By THYMOL MONK.

A STREET IN SUBURBIA. By E. W. PUGH.

THE NEW MOON. By C. E. RAIMOND.

MILLY'S STORY. By Mrs. MONTAGUE CRACKANTHORPE.

MRS. MUSGRAVE — AND HER HUSBAND. By RICHARD MARSH.

THE RED BADGE OF COURAGE. By STEPHEN CRANE.

THE DEMAGOGUE AND LADY PHAYRE. By WILLIAM J. LOCKE.

HER OWN DEVICES. By C. G. COMPTON.

PAPIER MACHÉ. By CHARLES ALLEN.

THE NEW VIRTUE. By Mrs. OSCAR BERINGER.

ACROSS AN ULSTER BOG. By M. HAMILTON.

ONE OF GOD'S DILEMMAS. By ALLEN UPWARD.

Other Volumes to follow.

UNIFORM EDITION OF

THE NOVELS OF BJÖRNSTJERNE BJORNSON

Edited by EDMUND GOSSE.

Fcap. 8vo, cloth, 3s. net each Volume.

Vol. I.—SYNNÖVÉ SOLBAKKEN.

With Introductory Essay by EDMUND GOSSE, and a Portrait of the Author.

Vol. II.—ARNE.
Vol. III.—A HAPPY BOY.

To be followed by

IV. THE FISHER LASS.
V. THE BRIDAL MARCH AND A DAY.

VI. MAGNHILD AND DUST
VII. CAPTAIN MANSANA AND MOTHER'S HANDS.

VIII. ABSALOM'S HAIR, AND A PAINFUL MEMORY.

UNIFORM EDITION OF

THE NOVELS OF IVAN TURGENEV.

Translated by CONSTANCE GARNETT.

Fcap. 8vo, cloth, price, 3s. net each Volume.

Vol. I.—RUDIN.

With a Portrait of the Author and an Introduction by STEPNIAK.

Vol. II.—A HOUSE OF GENTLEFOLK.

Vol. III.—ON THE EVE.

Vol. IV.—FATHERS AND CHILDREN.

Vol. V.—SMOKE.

Vol. VI., VII.—VIRGIN SOIL. (Two Volumes.)

Vol. VIII., IX.—A SPORTSMAN'S SKETCHES.
(Two Volumes).

Heinemann's International Library.

EDITED BY EDMUND GOSSE

New Review.—"If you have any pernicious remnants of iterary chauvinism I hope it will not survive the series of foreign classics of which Mr. William Heinemann, aided by Mr. Edmund Gosse, is publishing translations to the great contentment of all lovers of literature."

Each Volume has an Introduction specially written by the Editor.

Price, in paper covers, 2s. 6d. each; or cloth, 3s. 6d.

IN GOD'S WAY. From the Norwegian of BJÖRNSTJERNE BJÖRNSON.

PIERRE AND JEAN. From the French of GUY DE MAUPASSANT.

THE CHIEF JUSTICE. From the German of KARL EMIL FRANZOS, Author of "For the Right," &c.

WORK WHILE YE HAVE THE LIGHT. From the Russian of Count LEO TOLSTOY.

FANTASY. From the Italian of MATILDE SERAO.

FROTH. From the Spanish of Don ARMANDO PALACIO-VALDÉS.

FOOTSTEPS OF FATE. From the Dutch of LOUIS COUPERUS.

PEPITA JIMÉNEZ. From the Spanish of JUAN VALERA.

THE COMMODORE'S DAUGHTERS. From the Norwegian of JONAS LIE.

THE HERITAGE OF THE KURTS. From the Norwegian of BJÖRNSTJERNE BJÖRNSON.

LOU. From the German of BARON ALEXANDER VON ROBERTS.

DOÑA LUZ. From the Spanish of JUAN VALERA.

THE JEW. From the Polish of JOSEPH IGNATIUS KRASZEWSKI.

UNDER THE YOKE. From the Bulgarian of IVAN VAZOFF.

FAREWELL LOVE! From the Italian of MATILDE SERAO.

THE GRANDEE. From the Spanish of Don ARMANDO PALACIO-VALDÉS.

A COMMON STORY. From the Russian of GONTCHAROFF.

WOMAN'S FOLLY. From the Italian of GEMMA FERRUGGIA.

SIREN VOICES (NIELS LYHNË). From the Danish of J. G. JACOBSEN.

In preparation.

NIOBE. From the Norwegian of JONAS LIE.

popular 3s. 6d. Novels.

THE REDS OF THE MIDI, an Episode of the French Revolution. Translated from the Provençal of Félix Gras. By Mrs. CATHERINE A. JANVIER.

ELI'S DAUGHTER. By J. H. PEARCE, Author of "Inconsequent Lives."

INCONSEQUENT LIVES. A Village Chronicle. By J. H. PEARCE, Author of "Esther Pentreath," &c.

HER OWN FOLK. (En Famille.) By HECTOR MALOT, Author of "No Relations." Translated by Lady MARY LOYD.

CAPT'N DAVY'S HONEYMOON, The Blind Mother, and The Last Confession. By HALL CAINE, Author of "The Bondman," "The Scapegoat," &c.

A MARKED MAN: Some Episodes in his Life. By ADA CAMBRIDGE, Author of "A Little Minx," "The Three Miss Kings," "Not All in Vain," &c.

THE THREE MISS KINGS. By ADA CAMBRIDGE.

A LITTLE MINX. By ADA CAMBRIDGE.

NOT ALL IN VAIN. By ADA CAMBRIDGE.

A KNIGHT OF THE WHITE FEATHER. By TASMA, Author of "The Penance of Portia James," "Uncle Piper of Piper's Hill," &c.

UNCLE PIPER OF PIPER'S HILL. By TASMA.

THE PENANCE OF PORTIA JAMES. By TASMA.

THE COPPERHEAD; and other Stories of the North during the American War. By HAROLD FREDERIC, Author of "The Return of the O'Mahony," "In the Valley," &c.

THE RETURN OF THE O'MAHONY. By HAROLD FREDERIC, Author of "In the Valley," &c. With Illustrations.

IN THE VALLEY. By HAROLD FREDERIC, Author of "The Lawton Girl," "Seth's Brother's Wife," &c. With Illustrations.

THE SURRENDER OF MARGARET BELLARMINE. By ADELINE SERGEANT, Author of "The Story of a Penitent Soul."

THE STORY OF A PENITENT SOUL. Being the Private Papers of Mr. Stephen Dart, late Minister at Lynnbridge, in the County of Lincoln. By ADELINE SERGEANT, Author of "No Saint," &c.

THE O'CONNORS OF BALLINAHINCH. By Mrs. HUNGERFORD, Author of "Molly Bawn," &c.

NOR WIFE, NOR MAID. By Mrs. HUNGERFORD, Author of "Molly Bawn," &c.

THE HOYDEN. By Mrs. HUNGERFORD.

MAMMON. A Novel. By Mrs. ALEXANDER, Author of "The Wooing O't," &c.

DAUGHTERS OF MEN. By HANNAH LYNCH, Author of "The Prince of the Glades," &c.

Popular 3s. 6d. Novels.

THE TOWER OF TADDEO. By OUIDA, Author of "Two Little Wooden Shoes," &c. New Edition.

AVENGED ON SOCIETY. By H. F. WOOD, Author of "The Englishman of the Rue Cain," "The Passenger from Scotland Yard

APPASSIONATA : A Musician's Story. By ELSA D'ESTERRE KEELING.

A COMEDY OF MASKS. By ERNEST DOWSON and ARTHUR MOORE.

A ROMANCE OF THE CAPE FRONTIER. By BERTRAM MITFORD, Author of "Through the Zulu Country," &c.

'TWEEN SNOW AND FIRE. A Tale of the Kafir War of 1877. By BERTRAM MITFORD.

ORIOLE'S DAUGHTER. By JESSIE FOTHERGILL, Author of "The First Violin," &c.

THE MASTER OF THE MAGICIANS. By ELIZABETH STUART PHELPS and HERBERT D. WARD.

THE HEAD OF THE FIRM. By Mrs. RIDDELL, Author of "George Geith," "Maxwell Drewett," &c.

A CONSPIRACY OF SILENCE. By G. COLMORE, Author of "A Daughter of Music," &c.

A DAUGHTER OF MUSIC. By G. COLMORE, Author of "A Conspiracy of Silence."

ACCORDING TO ST. JOHN. By AMÉLIE RIVES, Author of "The Quick or the Dead."

KITTY'S FATHER. By FRANK BARRETT, Author of "The Admirable Lady Biddy Fane," &c.

THE JUSTIFICATION OF ANDREW LEBRUN. By F. BARRETT.

A QUESTION OF TASTE. By MAARTEN MAARTENS, Author of "An Old Maid's Love," &c.

COME LIVE WITH ME AND BE MY LOVE. By ROBERT BUCHANAN, Author of "The Moment After," "The Coming Terror," &c.

DONALD MARCY. By ELIZABETH STUART PHELPS, Author of "The Gates Ajar," &c.

IN THE DWELLINGS OF SILENCE. A Romance of Russia. By WALKER KENNEDY.

LOS CERRITOS. A Romance of the Modern Time. By GERTRUDE FRANKLIN ATHERTON, Author of "Hermia Suydam," and "What Dreams may Come."

Short Stories in One Volume.

Three Shillings and Sixpence each.

WRECKAGE, and other Stories. By HUBERT CRACKAN-
THORPE. Second Edition.

MADEMOISELLE MISS, and other Stories. By HENRY
HARLAND, Author of "Mea Culpa," &c.

THE ATTACK ON THE MILL, and other Sketches
of War. By EMILE ZOLA. With an Essay on the short stories of M.
Zola by EDMUND GOSSE.

THE AVERAGE WOMAN. By WOLCOTT BALESTIER.
With an Introduction by HENRY JAMES.

BLESSED ARE THE POOR. By FRANÇOIS COPPÉE.
With an Introduction by T. P. O'CONNOR.

PERCHANCE TO DREAM, and other Stories. By MAR-
GARET S. BRISCOE.

WRECKERS AND METHODISTS. Cornish Stories. By
H. D. LOWRY.

Popular Shilling Books.

PRETTY MISS SMITH. By FLORENCE WARDEN, Author
of "The House on the Marsh," "A Witch of the Hills," &c.

MADAME VALERIE. By F. C. PHILIPS, Author of "As
in a Looking-Glass," &c.

THE MOMENT AFTER: A Tale of the Unseen. By
ROBERT BUCHANAN.

CLUES; or, Leaves from a Chief Constable's Note-Book.
By WILLIAM HENDERSON, Chief Constable of Edinburgh.

THE NORTH AMERICAN REVIEW.

Edited by LLOYD BRYCE.

Published monthly.   Price 2s. 6d.

THE NEW REVIEW.

NEW SERIES.

Edited by W. E. HENLEY.

Published Monthly, price 1s.

LONDON:
WILLIAM HEINEMANN,
21 BEDFORD STREET, W.C.